BRIGHT CITY

By: dc edwards

Bright City
By
dc edwards

DEDICATION

For You:

The moon of my life

The lunch dates

The hustlers

The artists who aren't starving

The ending of one life and the beginning of the next

.

TABLE OF CONTENTS

DEDICATION iii

ACKNOWLEDGMENTS.. vi

Chapter One... 8

Chapter Two 24

Chapter Three.. 33

Chapter Four 40

Chapter Five 49

Chapter Six 59

Chapter Seven... 67

Chapter Eight 76

Chapter Nine... 90

Chapter Ten 102

Chapter Eleven 113

Chapter Twelve... 119

Chapter Thirteen 124

Chapter Fourteen 131

Chapter Fifteen... 138

Chapter Sixteen 146

BRIGHT CITY

Chapter Seventeen.. 156

Chapter Eighteen.. 164

Chapter Nineteen.. 172

Chapter Twenty... 185

Chapter Twenty-One.. 191

Chapter Twenty-Two 196

Chapter Twenty-Three.. 211

Chapter Twenty-Four 220

Chapter Twenty-Five 229

Chapter Twenty-Six 239

Chapter Twenty-Seven.. 245

Chapter Twenty-Eight 253

Epilogue.. 259

ACKNOWLEDGMENTS

Bright City started off as a genetically engineered vampire travel story with Abigail at its helm. Thankfully, she decided that we should go in a different direction. She didn't need vampires in her life, she needed a fiery red-head and a revolution. I'd like to also thank my long-lost sister Kendra Reeves, who decided I was not too much of a stranger to take a chance on introducing me to her publisher. Best present, ever! Thanks to Latoya Chandler, publisher extraordinaire and probably the most patient person that has ever walked the planet. Thank you for waiting for me to heal from 2016 to push the rest of this book onto your plate. Also, thanks to everyone that works with Passion Publication (editors and designers) I appreciate all of your work and the cover for this book is perfect! To my "big brother," one of my favorite poets, and brilliant editor, Micheal Kleber-Diggs. I can't tell you how much I have appreciated all your labor on my manuscripts, listening to me whine about my inability to write, and swooping in at the right time to push me to dig into my spirit just when I need it. I thank the Universe that we met.

Finally, I want to thank Anitra Cottledge. My love, my best friend, my world. Writing for you, the moon of my life, is a pleasure. Thank you for being my biggest fan, the perfect critic and the best audience a frequently-writing-blocked author could have.

BRIGHT CITY

CHAPTER ONE

❧ • ❦

I **RUN BY THE PYRAMIDS OF GIZA** every morning at 8 am. I jog up the trail anticipating their imposing size as the sun rises behind them. I usually love the burn in my thighs, but today it's an annoyance. I pull up the hood on my thermo suit and set it to cool. I'm eager to turn the next bend and away from the harsh sun. The exile of a group of dissidents is in two days. I grew up with the three of them. One of them is my best friend, Katherine Floyd. Katherine has always been a rebel, always talking about the inequities in our Colony, in our Kingdom. Now I have to take the stand against her. I have to sentence her to the Outlands. Katherine has been my best friend since I could remember. There's no way she could be a traitor. Our lives have required devotion to this Colony. She comes from one of the founding family's lineage. Still, I turn memories over in my mind searching for some indication that she would betray the Colony. I can't find any and I kick myself for even trying to.

By 8:30, I turn past the largest of the pyramids and slow my pace as the sand hardens into cobblestones. I flip down my hood and set the suit to warm as the chill of alleys between patisseries and coffee shops hits my face. I am glad that graffiti I encountered last week is gone.

A chilly wind blows off the Seine just as I pass by the Eiffel Tower. I stop by its edge to catch my breath and tie my shoe. I touch the wet cobblestone, and the gritty, dark dirt between my fingers drags me back to the day of Katherine's arrest. I was on a tracking mission headed towards the shacks.

The small two-room houses are like human-sized traps with indoor facilities; they are old but in good shape. Wandering Outlanders use them for temporary shelter. We're then able to tranquilize them and track them. We take tissue and blood samples to figure out where they're from, what diseases they may be carrying and to determine lineage. The Colony has millions of strands of DNA. We use the samples to create vaccines for the Colonies. We're preserving the DNA of millions of people who would eventually die out without our help. So we cleanse the DNA, and when we find matches of families that have been disconnected we inject them with parts of the strand so that they can be healthy enough to maintain their lineage. Without us, the people in the Outlands would die.

"Approaching the shacks," I said on the day of Katherine's arrest. I remember moving through tall grass towards the small structures.

"Heat signatures indicate three bodies; two adults, one child," Katherine said through my earpiece.

"Gas them in 3…2…1."

"Gas released. Body temperature decreased. Sleep stasis achieved."

9

"Moving in."

I walked in the house and found a little girl curled up in a large chair next to the window, an adult male subject at the kitchenette table and an adult female subject on the couch. I quickly opened my bag and began harvesting samples from the adult male before moving on to the adult female.

"Abby, leave the kid alone."

"Katherine, I have to get samples from her too."

"C'mon Abs. This job is fucking weird right?"

"It's my job. And it's your job to process this material," I said as I pressed my palm to a brick on the wall. The block glowed green with my handprint. Parts of the wall next to my handprint slid away revealing the processing station. A viewer across the wall flickered alive, and I smiled when Katherine popped onto the screen. I convinced her to be my six on this trip. In the past, she refused to do the Comm for DNA collections. She'd called it inhumane. I had hoped she would change her mind. I hated using other Comm engineers on those trips.

"I can't do this," Katherine said.

"You knew I was going out to do this today," I said.

"Can I ask you a question?"

"Process blood vial XY One and I'll answer."
I watched her fingers slide across her screen; then I prepped the other two slides for processing.

"XY One completed; traces of Dank Plague virus. Looks like he's just a carrier, though. High blood pressure and he might have the beginnings of the flu. Recommendations," Katherine responded.

"Eh, none," I said slipping another slide into the processor.

"Abs, dude might have the flu, high blood pressure and is carrying the Dank Plague virus and no recommendations?"

I was pissed. I am the Tracker. I make the decisions. Besides we were going to tag them anyway.

"Negative, let's look at XX One and then the girl to see if we have any later recommendations."

"Screw that, Abs, give him some antibiotics at least for the flu."

"Negative. What's your question?"

"You answered it already," she said, as two antibiotic vials dropped into the delivery tray.

"I didn't authorize this. And what do you mean I answered it."

"I was gonna ask if you have any compassion."

"For the Outlanders? Seriously Katherine, why do you think I'm out here?"

"You're experimenting that's what."

"Yes, to make their lives better."

"Not if you deny them treatment."

"I'm not refusing treatment! I'm making an educated determination based on the findings from the blood and tissue samples."

"The people outside our walls are dying."

"How do you know? You've never been out there."

"I know more than you think, and you are the one who is blind to the truth about these experiments."

I moved over to the small girl and drew blood from her. I remember thinking she had a beautiful face, no scars on her freshly scrubbed brown skin and seemed healthy. I thought how that's somewhat rare for a kid in the Outlands. Most kids outside of our walls are rough.

"Process XX Two, and we're finished."

"Abby I have to tell you something."

"What? That you want me to give them antibiotics? Fine, Katherine if it'll get you off my back. Three vials; adjust dosage to gender and weight. I'll need three sub-muscle tracer devices too. These three are pretty well fed I wanna see where they go."

"Done," she said as the vials slid into the tray, "Listen, Abby, I have to tell you something."

"Let me just do these injections."

"No, Abs listen."

I remember hearing the clanking through my earpiece and the look on Katherine's face as she turned to look at the door of her Communications cell to the viewer.

"What's happening over there?"

"They're coming for me," she said.

"Who's coming for you," I yelled.

"Listen to me; these experiments are part of a conspiracy…"

I called out to her and then the message appeared across the viewer:

Vice Regent Drexler, your Comm Operator, is unavailable. Please connect to the central server for completion of experiment 183. Once complete please terminate further initiatives and return to base. Copy.

Distant gunshots snatch me back as I trip over jagged cobblestones and crash to the muddied ground. My breath comes out in puffs of white as I push myself up and jog towards the Arc d' Triomphe. I look around and notice for the first time that it's curiously silent. A shrieking siren pierces the silence. People begin streaming out of the buildings screaming and yelling in rapid French. I'm shoved between them, pushed off my path and into an alley.

"Computer," I say, "analyze program 321: Morning Marathon."

321: Morning Marathon analysis complete, no anomalies detected, responds the female computerized voice.

A shrill squeal rises above the thunderous stampede of people culminating in an explosion. I'm thrown against one of the walls in the alley as bricks and glass slice through the nearest people.

"Computer, run the program through again," I say, pressing myself tight against a wall as a near pitch-black darkness descends around me.

321: Morning Marathon analysis shows no anomalies.

"Computer, examine historical chronology."

I pull myself up and peek around the corner. I see families and soldiers running through the streets. White spots of rapid gunfire, like raining stars, split the dark black skies. I duck behind a teetering tower of boxes marked "fruit."

321: Morning Marathon analysis historical chronology: May 15, 1940, The Battle of France.

I look up and see artillery blasts shoot across the blackened sky.

"Alert Regent Drexler," I say.

I make a break towards a ruined building. French and German voices are yelling, issuing orders, and cursing the night. The voices rise around me like bleeps against the squawking bombing sirens and popping gunshots. That's

when I see the Panzer tanks rolling through the devastation.
The imposing monsters shake the ground; the walls tremble
as they approach. I hear the screech of a bomb overhead, as
I crash into a wall. I wipe the dust from my face. Blood
covers my hand. I sprint towards a crumbling building and
hide behind a barely standing wall. My breath comes out in
clouds as I watch the German storm troopers lock step
through the devastated streets. Seemingly ripped from
nightmares: creased and crisp uniforms bearing the
swastika, their black leather boots gleaming as if they were
shined just for this invasion, high cheekbones and thin
patrician noses on expressionless, pale faces.

"Abigail."

"Dad," I whisper.

"The dissidents must have gotten into your program."

"I think this isn't the first time," I say.

"The engineer told me you've been having some
irregularities for weeks," he responds.

"Yeah, I saw graffiti on the walls last week."

"A message."

"Nothing like this one."

"We can't get a lock on which program you're using,"
he says.

"I'm using the 60-minute 321: Morning Marathon, but
there might be some bleeding between this one and my 70-
minute program," I say as I creep through the building

avoiding broken glass and trash on the floor.

"Got it. Yes, there's some bleeding. You're in a section of France that you have in your 70-minute program. You're right at 55 minutes, but we'll see if we can get it shut down faster."

"Ah crap," I say as buildings begin to dissolve around me.

"We broke in, but you have to get out of there. Head towards the door at the end of the hallway. Go now!"

Air raid sirens blare above rumbling tanks, and I break out in a full sprint towards the door at the end of a collapsing hallway. A blast of heat pushes me through the door, and I tumble to a stop in front of a large cement wall with barbed wire twisting its way over the top. The streets are quiet and repaired but desolate. I know this wall from our history classes. I walk along the length of it touching its cold, smooth surface. I see the sign first, East and West Berlin. I frown as disembodied red writing scrawls along the side of the wall: *The Colony is Prison*. The program disintegrates around me, and the Holocise track comes into view. I tap on the data pad next to the exit and slip between the sliding doors of the disinfectant chamber. The hot spray of water and medicine peels my synthetic body suit from my skin washing it down the drain to repurposing itself the next morning.

I have to see Katherine. Inserting a battle simulation in my training program, live ammunition, and everything is her way of getting my attention.

"Computer, final landscape please," I say.

BRIGHT CITY

I lean against the wall; my head pressed to the glass, and breathe in the menthol tasting air that fogs up around me. I watch the hologram of a reflective lake flow like steam onto the glass door. It's backed by snowcapped mountains and green meadows.

I call Colony One in the Drexler Kingdom home. The Outlanders call us moles because we live underground; miles underground. Our home is a system of reinforced steel and concrete that can withstand nearly any type of weapon.

All of the Colonies in the Drexler Kingdom share a similar maze of advanced underground living areas. On the surface, 20 feet tall concrete and reinforced steel walls surround the average looking towns. There are ranch-style houses, a small grocery store, a mini strip mall with different storefront options, a small community clinic and a town hall. Most of the colonists used to live above ground, but we prepared for The Fall. Modeled after underground military bunkers that can hold thousands of people, the city we've created under the surface rivals once-great above-ground cities. With training facilities, a school, living pods, farms and recreational centers for social gatherings, our city thrives within its cold concrete walls.

The spray bandage tingles on my cheek, I feel my skin weave back together. I see my face reflected in an exposed piece of metal near the entrance, and the bruise is fading as quickly as it appeared. I rub away lotion from the bridge of my sparsely freckled nose and wipe away the excess lip gloss from my full lips. I'd heal in an hour.

The command center is bustling with activity. I remember when I was a kid my father called this the heart of the Colony. I was fascinated with the multiple screens that monitored most every area of our Colony. I know the function for each knob and colored light. Back then; I just thought they were pretty. Back then, I wondered at the energy in this place. I used to sneak into the command center and hide under my father's desk. I'd watch him move effortlessly through the bustling room. His reserved attitude in our living pod clashed with the passionate man in the command center. The citizens assigned to the command center looked at him with awe. He was badass: giving orders, solving problems, fixing panels. I was jealous of the time they got to spend with this man who rarely showed up in our family pod. So I resolved to become one of them when I got older.

I've always thought my father was tall. Now as I approach him, pulling my curling hair off my collar as per regulations, I realize that my eyes are just above his shoulders. I feel myself slouching, and I pull up to my full 5'10" height. I adjust the zipper on the jacket of my creased formal navy blue uniform. I think back to when I was thirteen, when I was tall and thin and rangy, all arms and legs. I was taller than all the other kids in my cohort, so I slouched a lot. My father would scold me; remind me I'm the future Regent. He often advised that because I am the next in line to lead our Colony, our Kingdom, bearing the title Vice Regent, means being watched all the time. He reminded me that colonists would look to me as their future Regent; therefore I must always be aware and exhibit the doctrine of our society. He reminded me that I have to set an example. He reminded me that we are no longer in the times before The Fall that women are not objects. All of us are superior individuals. We stand tall. Although his speeches were epic, they didn't stop me from slouching.

"Regent Drexler, I…"

I wait. He does this. He makes me wait until he's finished signing forms or typing out emails before hearing me out. He says waiting, and patience creates great leaders. I hate waiting. Still, I stand with my hands behind my back, at attention, stiff and attempting to ignore the tech crew in the command center.

"I know. You want to talk more about Katherine," he says, as he presses his thumb to a data pad, his signature on some document.

"Yes, I think she knows something."

"Your friend is a traitor to our Kingdom and all the Colonies within it. She wants to destroy what The Prophet, your many time's great-grandfathers, struggled to build."

"No disrespect, sir, but I disagree."

I stare into his cobalt gray eyes, mirror images of my own. Usually, I back down. His glares have been known to wither dissent. But I knew what happened in my Holocise program was Katherine's cry for help.

"Explain."

"I just...I just know her, Regent Drexler. She's my best friend."

"And she's spent more time in ReEducation – learning and relearning our laws – than any child born in this Colony. Because she's your friend, we protected her. But this time it's not some childish prank. She is a criminal, a traitor."

"Why is she a traitor? Is she a traitor because she

wants to change in our Colony?" I ask, following him as he moves from one station to another.

"Abigail, The Prophet intentionally removed our people from the old world where people were starving, where individuals who looked different were hated and vilified. He created the world that shielded us from that, which also protected us from its destruction. Why would anyone from our Kingdom want to live in a world where rape and murder and theft are regular occurrences? It's ridiculous."

"It's true that The Outlands are full of starving people. And it's also true that there is still theft and murder. But we aren't like them. We should listen to her concerns."

"The people out there didn't learn the lessons of The Fall. In here, we are consistently creating a better world. There is freedom, but there is also treason. She has the freedom to speak, but she does not have the freedom to destroy our way of life."

"And yet, with all due respect sir, we go out there and observe and collect for our benefit. If we are creating a better world why aren't we doing it out there? I think that is something Katherine wants to know," I say.

"We don't create anything for them because those people out there are the descendants of the people who destroyed the world. And those people out there would tear our world apart if they had a chance."

"Yes, I know, but…"

"You are a Vice Regent. This conversation is basic history from your seventh-year classes. Are you so caught up in your emotions for your friend that you forget everything that you know about the outside world?"

I sigh, shift my stance, and try not to scratch at the wound on my cheek. I know he's right. We learned how horrible the world was before The Fall: the inequality between people, the poverty, the racism, and bigotry of every sort. Crime and fear were part of everyday life. It was The Prophet, Dr. Alfred Drexler, who started the first Colony in a little town in the south. He'd worked on the hydrogen bomb that destroyed Nagasaki and Hiroshima. He believed hate would destroy the world. So he bought a small struggling town in the South; he convinced black and white folks to live together in peace and created the first of ten Colonies in what would become the Drexton Kingdom, known before The Fall as Drexton Incorporated. And he was right; over a century ago, when they got the chance, the world, both allies, and enemies, hunted the United States. They took advantage of America's crippled systems after the Dank Plague killed millions. The Dank Plague was the government's most successful foray into genetic assassination or what they used to call eugenics. Scientists managed to create a genetic switch in HIV.

This way if it came into contact with a particular gene in the host's body it would "switch on" and rapidly kill the person. Considered a success until it started killing almost everyone who came in contact with it, regardless genetic switch. Natural disasters compounded the destruction as they tore through the remaining major cities. Then the drones came. They flooded the country. Allies and enemies alike placed crushing sanctions on imports, virtually starving the survivors of the Dank Plague.

The neighbors who left them alone in the past overran the Colonies without walls. Other Colonies couldn't stop the spread of the Plague through their colonists who were leaving the compound to help the afflicted. We call the end of the United States "The Fall." And after The Fall only four Colonies remain in the Kingdom. Three colonies are in the former southern US and my Colony, in the North. We are connected now only by a complicated Internet satellite hybrid. But I can't believe the rumors I'm hearing; that Katherine participated in a terrorist action against the Kingdom. And of course, because of this severe infraction, only the ReEducation team has been allowed to see her. Still, I hope this is just one of her practical jokes gone awry. It has happened before.

"She's young," I reply, following him as he walks out of a sliding door and into the hallway.

"You're young. Half of the techs and the people on my staff are her age as well. And yet, none of them seem to want to bring the past into our world."

I stop following him as he passes by a mural of an orange sunrise, a group of children painted years ago along the brightly lit hallway walls. He doesn't notice until he's halfway towards the elevator.

"Sir, I want to speak to you as your daughter."

He moves closer to me, hands stuffed in his pockets, frown lines deepen his handsome brown face. Mirror images, I think. My mother used to call us that. Mirror images. Both of us brown skinned, the color of her favorite caramel, she'd say. Both of us having the same black curly hair. Mine in a bun above my collar, his speckled gray, short on the sides, and curly on top. Same freely-given broad smile. But he doesn't smile like he used to. Like he did before Mom's death. Neither do I.

"Do it quickly," he replies.

I struggle for the words. How do I explain that I know Katherine is guilty of something but not what she's accused? That I know her desire to want this so-called freedom comes with a price. And that all I want to do is talk her out of whatever she's gotten herself involved with, get her to admit that she's wrong. She's always been a hell raiser. He's right; she's spent more time in the ReEducation center than anyone I've ever known. But it's all innocent fun. I just want to bring her back to us; someone or something has corrupted her. I just want to give her a chance to explain. How can I say all this, as he's staring at me, his mind made up that she's a traitor?

"I want to see her. I need to see her. We're like sisters. She's my best friend, Daddy."

"Abigail, honey," he places his palms on my shoulders, and I feel the tension seep from them, "I appreciate how you feel, but my answer is no."

CHAPTER TWO

❧ • ❧

I **THINK ABOUT MY CONVERSATION WITH** my father as I pass a group of children on their way to their combat training class. The group of ten boys and girls salutes me; quickly placing their backs against a brightly colored mural along a concrete wall, their small fingers pressed against their foreheads. I smile and nod at them before they scurry away, voices elevated as they chatter amongst one another.

Katherine always hated saluting. For years, we argued about it. I know my father's justification for justice above all is important. We cannot have a truly working society if any one of us is privileged above others. I know this. But I can't help feeling like I'm giving up on Katherine.

I hurry blindly through the halls, passing meeting rooms and training areas. Today, I'm eager to teach my class on Historical Realism. In it, we discuss the raw facts of the society before The Fall and how learning from the past helps us maintain societal rules. I pause in front of the door to the classroom. Designed in the style of pre-Fall classrooms, chairs, and desks line the front of the room in rows. The style is very different from the other open-style classes where the kids can sit anywhere they want. For this type of class, we want to show the challenges of the rigidity of the previous school system. It also forces students to challenge leadership in the classroom. We want them to see themselves as a collective, the good of the Colony above all. Old maps, images of the men who used to run the former United States cover the walls. The fake windows are image screens that show a bustling city beyond the classroom. I take a deep breath before opening the sliding door. I can hear their voices; the rise and fall of their chatter sometimes put me on edge. I prefer the outside to this assignment, but my father thought it was good for the Vice Regent to be seen in the Colony more than outside of it. He thought people would think I wouldn't be able to run the community when the time came if I wasn't seen interacting with the Colonists. I didn't agree, but it wasn't my choice. Still, I am lucky; the group of 10 kids is sharp and engaged. They like their studies and push me to challenge them. I take in another deep breath and place my hand on the pad next to the door that slides open.

"Tell her Vice Regent, tell her she's wrong!"

The door swishes shut behind me, and I face two factions. On one side of the classroom are 7 of the ten children; mostly boys and the other three children, all girls stand with their hands crossed and heads held high. In front of the smaller group is Harper. Harper is the reason I am always anxious about this class. She reminds me so much of Katherine. She's proud, fiercely intelligent and argumentative. It's exciting and frightening all at once.

"She cannot be just 'wrong.' If she is 'wrong' do you have concrete evidence? Also, do we accuse individuals of being 'wrong' without examining and interrogating that evidence?"

Dave, the ringleader of the larger group, immediately snaps to attention. He's the palest kid in the room with dirty blonde hair and green eyes. His sharp rare genetic patrician features contrast Harper's broad nose, full lips and the rich umber of her brown skin.

"No, ma'am but…"

"But?"

"But Harper is wrong Vice Regent."

"Harper?" I say as I wave everyone to their assigned seats.

Most of the students move to their desks. Harper, who recently had a growth spurt, now towers over her fellow students. She doesn't budge from the front of the classroom. I smile. I admire her strength of will. Much like I respect Katherine's. Katherine spent her 13th birthday in ReEducation. She questioned everything. Fear creeps up my spine as Harper shifts to stand behind the podium. Her stance, both hands on her developing hips, chin held high, and her steely resolve remind me of Katherine. I sit on the edge of my desk.

"Vice Regent, there is no doubt that our society was created to protect the good of the many, correct."

"Yes, that is the history."

"We claim to have effectively eliminated the problems of the old society from our Kingdom."

"Yes, what is your point?"

"But have we eliminated those elements or have we avoided them because of our genetic engineering? And most importantly, we have not removed classism; the old governments used to maintain authority. As you know, it also used divisive strategies to pit the less fortunate against each other so those with means could remain above the fray among those without."

"Where are you going with this Harper?"

"She thinks the people in ReEducation are right and we're traitors!" Dave shouts.

The room explodes with chatter. Harper slants her eyes at me and then at her fellow students. Katherine used to give me the same look when she didn't believe one of our instructors or when she didn't agree with the class material.

"Quiet everyone. Dave, another outburst like that and I'll send you to ReEducation."

"Now," I say as I turn towards Harper, "is that true? Do you believe the colonists in ReEducation are right in their attempted terrorism and we, the leaders of the Kingdom and specifically this Colony are traitors?"

"Yes."

The classroom let out a collective gasp and Dave raised his eyebrows at me pointing in Harper's direction with an I-told-you-so shrug.

"Why do you feel this way, Harper? Right now your

chance to argue your position without penalty."

"The governments before had leaders who rose above the ordinary people. Everyone listened to them. We have dozens of historical documents that point to how much they lied and manipulated the ordinary citizens. We talk about those lies and manipulations in this class. We mainly focus on the lies they told about The Fall, how it started, what caused it. We talk all the time about equity. But we do not live in an equitable environment. We can't. Someone has to be in charge. It only seems fair because of the space we share. But you, Vice Regent, have more power over anyone your age. Even the people who supposedly 'outrank' you have to answer to you if you demanded it."

"This may be a good argument for classism in our Kingdom, but these young people attempted to destroy our society."

"How do you know that? Have you seen any evidence?"

"No, but I trust it will be shown to us during the proceedings tomorrow."

"Why should I trust anything that the Council says or you or the Regent?" Harper asks.

Dave grunts his disapproval and the room go too silent.

"You trust us because we would do nothing to lead our Kingdom and this Colony, in particular, to ruin."

"How can we be sure, though? Back before The Fall most people distrusted the government but let it run their lives anyway. They had proof that nearly every level of government was corrupt, but they still made excuses. And yet, we colonists are supposed to trust you, the leaders because you tell us to. How do I know that whatever so-called evidence the Council presents isn't just made up? The leaders know the worst thing they could show the prisoners desire to destroy the Colony. Of course, Colonists would insist on exile, which is death. So even though we're against murder, we are essentially condemning them to death. Washing our hands of it and supposedly protecting the Colony and Kingdom. But we have no guarantee that they did anything wrong."

Dave's hand shoots up, waving vigorously. I nod in his direction. He's the odd boy out in the class. But many of the students look to him as a leader. His genetics are outdated. I remember when he was born my mother spent time in the lab with his blood work. My parents used to whisper that Dave's parents were surprised when their second son's pink skin clashed against their glowing copper complexions. I was only five years old, but even then I could tell the concern in their voices. Pale children are exceedingly rare in the Colony.

"Yes, Dave."

"Vice Regent, the leaders have the right to protect the people from information that could create panic and fear. They do not have the right to create information that would create panic and fear."

"This is very true. But I think what Harper might be saying is that to keep the Colonists docile the leaders would present information that would cause Colonists to protect the society. Am I right, Harper?"

"In a way, yes."

"But if that's what she's saying then she's committing treason," Dave says.

"Are you committing treason, Harper," I ask, hoping the girl will step away from her stance.

"If I say yes, then I'm going to ReEducation. If I say, no then I'm lying."

"Then you shouldn't say anything," I say to her.

Things eventually settle, and for the rest of the class, we study the fallout from 9/11. The simple one-note tone signaling the end of class drowns out the students. They quickly gather their belongings for their next class. Dave and two of his friends joke loudly about their next class; military training as the students walk out in pairs and triplets. Harper doesn't move.

"You are dismissed, Harper."

"You believe your best friend is a traitor?"

"She knows something and should therefore confess."

Harper cuts her long-lashed eyes at me and shakes her head. She goes to her desk and gathers her pack. I breathe a sigh of relief as she heads out the door. But before I could gather my thoughts, I look up to see her standing in the doorway.

"You are a coward, Vice Regent."

"I'm sorry?!"

BRIGHT CITY

"You are a coward."

"Harper, that is enough! I do not want to send you to ReEducation. You are in violation."

"She's your friend, Vice Regent. Do you know how many times we've all watched and admired the two of you? Dave used to admire Katherine. She was his favorite military instructor. Now he's calling her a traitor every five minutes. I don't believe it. Asking questions, demanding answers is not traitorous behavior."

"You don't know what she's done."

"Yeah and neither do you."

"That's all Harper. You're dismissed."

"Yes, Vice Regent!" Harper clicks her heels together and gives me a Nazi salute. Her arm stiffly extended before her, her hand a pointing slightly above my head. Her beautiful brown face filled with righteous anger. I gasp then leap to my feet, but before I could get to her, she runs out the door.

I slide into my chair and cry. Harper, with all her anger, is right. She's not misguided, though I'd love to paint her as just young and willful. The secret behind why Katherine and the two young men are in ReEducation haunts me. Whenever people are in ReEducation the reasons for being there are posted around the Colony. The community reconciles small infractions and larger ones. The Colonists in ReEducation are required to work with the community to resolve their violations; then they can be fully restored to the community. Very rarely are Colonists exiled. It had only happened once before when I was around nine years old. My parents talked about a man who had murdered his wife and child. It was a shock to the Colony. There was no other option for this murderer but exile.

I am concerned about Katherine's situation. If exile is a possibility, more than a possibility, then what did she do? What could they have possibly done that's worse than murder? Katherine is rebellious, but she's not a murderer. I think back to my conversation with my father. I know he's right that we should let the process determine the outcome. Harper also has a point that the Colonists have a right to the truth. And I know my friend. Katherine is many things, but a traitor isn't one of them. I can't imagine her doing anything that would destroy our life here. But I also know that she's probably hiding something. And she'll take that secret to the grave if the wrong person asks her. Maybe she reached out to me with that adolescent virus in my exercise program because I'm the only one she trusts.

"Damn it, Katherine," I say under my breath as I gather my things.

I have to meet with my father. I have to get him to see that she needs to talk to me; otherwise, Katherine is going to end up exiled, and I can't let that happen.

CHAPTER THREE

కా•ఆ

O
N THE WAY TO MY DAD'S POD, the family home
I left when I was 16, I try to think about what to say
to him. The walk gives me the best views of our
Colony. I pass by one of the many colorful murals in the
children's spaces and breathe the energy in the communal
areas. A couple of the Retribution soldiers pass me on their
way to the fighting ring; I let my mind wander to the rustic
beauty of the above ground homes of the Retribution
soldiers and elders. I never get tired of the beauty of our
home. As I pass by other pods, I can hear music and
laughter. Most windows have closed shades, but a few
people wave at me as I pass. When teens move out of our
family pods to begin our training, it can be exhilarating.
Adolescents are considered adults, so we spend lots of time
in a designated co-ed training space together. As children,
we spend so much time with our parents that we welcome
freedom.

But for me, the first days of living in my pod was
isolating. Katherine ran wild, of course. She spent long
nights hanging out with our friends, played at romance with
some of the older boys and girls, and spent a lot of time in

the fighting ring. Katherine loves her freedom and when we had down time, rarely spent time with her family. Early on, she wanted to be a Tracker, like me but later decided her tastes ran more towards Communications, which suited me just fine. If she'd been a Tracker, we wouldn't have been able to spend a lot of time together. Her being in Comm meant we could spend days together. Now is supposed to be the best time of our lives.

I stop just short of my father's pod. I can see the Winston's across the hallway through their window. Layla, their daughter, is a year behind Katherine and me. She's going to be an excellent Tracker. I put my hand to the panel next to the door and hear a muffled beep on the other side. The door slides open, and my father's stern face greets me.

"Are you ok," he asks, his body blocking the view of the room.

"Yes, I just hoped we could have dinner together."

"Oh, yeah, sorry forgive my manners," he says, as he steps aside.

The common room looks the same; cluttered with charts and books, a stack of dishes in the sink, and clothes piled in a basket in the corner. My father was always a great cook, and tonight is no exception. A pot of chili is heating on the stove, but his single bowl and spoon on the table next to his journal look lonely. I know that he often has colleagues over for dinner. He uses those evenings for strategizing, but I think it's because he hates silence.

"No guests?"

"I needed some quiet."

BRIGHT CITY

"I'm sorry," I say.

He pulls me into an embrace then kisses my forehead. I chuckle and hug him back.

"I'm starving," he says.

"Yeah, me too!"

He places an overflowing bread basket, steam rising from the freshly baked sourdough, on the table. The basket is an heirloom, woven from dried corn husks, passed through our family from before my father was born. My dad places a bowl of chili in front of me and begins to talk about his day. He tells me about a kid on his team who misread the radar and mistook a dog for a car. He laughs when he relays the story. His laugh is powerful, right from his gut. For a long time after Mom died, neither of us could smile. Sometimes it seems like he still can't find his. I relax into my chair; like when I was a kid. Back when we knew each other well, I was never afraid to talk to him. Now I can't gauge him.

"How is your class going," he asks between bites of bread and butter.

"My class is conflicted about tomorrow."

"What about tomorrow," he asks as he pulls apart a piece of bread and dips it in his chili.

"They are conflicted about the Mediation tomorrow."

"Mmmhmm."

"Well, some of them believe that the young people in ReEducation are traitors, but there are others who don't see it that way."

"And you told them?"

"I let them debate it. It's good for my students to work through their thoughts."

"But I'm sure you told them that the Council would make the best decision based on the evidence."

"Of course but…"

"You are in charge of young minds, Abigail. It's important for you to remember that."

"I do, of course, sir. I do but…"

"Do you know what I did with that young man who mistook a dog for a car?"

"No, sir, I don't."

"He went to ReEducation."

"Why?"

"He was sent to ReEducation because he could not accept that what he did could have cost many lives. He is a decent specialist; great even. But even the great ones falter. His mistake caused undo momentary panic. Do you know that the young man mobilized the Retribution soldiers in that area of the wall before even sending a team to investigate? There was a Tracker in the field. He had multiple ways of approaching this problem, and he panicked. We can't have people running amok. There are lives at stake. That is the lesson that your class needed to learn today. That no matter what these young traitors in ReEducation believed was happening it was unnecessary for them to take matters into their hands."

I place my spoon next to my half empty bowl and rub my temples. It's all such a big mess in my head.

"I'd like to plead Katherine's case," I say pushing forward.

"I figured as much."

"She's young. All three of them are young."

"That specialist is young. Youth has nothing to do with it. And using that as an excuse is beneath you. We are a young Colony. Are you too young to go out into the Outlands? Are many of your friends who are Retribution soldiers too young to live above? No, of course not."

"It's not necessarily about their youth making them incapable of making decisions, sir, it's about the fact that sometimes young people are impulsive."

"Proving my point of why I sent that specialist to ReEducation. We don't have the luxury of impulsiveness. You know this," he says, before wiping his mouth with a napkin and getting up to rinse his bowl out in the sink.

"Katherine has always been impulsive which makes her an excellent Comm. And a great friend," I insist.

"Are you pleading for her or are you pleading for all of them?"

"Her, of course."

"Is that just? They are all accused of the same crime, and you grew up with all three of them. You are all the same age. What makes Katherine so unique?"

"She's my best friend. She's like my sister."

"But is what you're doing right here, right now equitable? The boys' families would want to come and have dinner with me and plead for their sons. They can't. Katherine's mother cannot come in here and ask for leniency. You are using our familial relationship unjustly. It's wrong."

"But…"

"No buts, Abigail. Justice will prevail."

"How can justice prevail when I'm the only one who can get through to Katherine? I'm the only one who can make her tell the truth."

"Katherine is young, but she is an adult. She has to be accountable for her actions. That is the reality of all of this, Abigail. Don't let your love for your friend outweigh the good of the Colony, of the Kingdom!"

I stand up and head towards the door. I want to scream at my Dad, force him to back down. I breathe in deeply and push the tears back from the corners of my eyes.

"You will obey me, Abigail. I do not permit you to see Katherine. You are Vice Regent of Drexler Colony Number One. You have to be accountable to all the people, not just your friend."

BRIGHT CITY

I turn to face him and think about Harper and her anger with me this afternoon. I realize that she's right. There is loyalty to the Colony and the Kingdom, but there's also loyalty to my friend. And I know I can help them.

"Yes, sir," I say.

CHAPTER FOUR

&•&

I **STEP OUT OF AN ELEVATOR TWO STORIES** below the Command Center and into the ReEducation Center hallway. In this place, there are no children in bright clothing running from class to class. No intricately drawn murals depicting the history of the Kingdom. It's quiet down here. The only sound is the air-filtration system quietly whooshing every few seconds through the stark white hallway.

"Vice Regent Abigail Drexler," I announce into the speaker. I press my hand to the identification pad. My fingerprints bloom a bright green across the screen.

The door slides open revealing my Dad's most trusted advisor, Warren Peters. His reptilian smile has always made my stomach churn. Today is no different.

"Vice Regent," he tilts his head in a slight nod, "Welcome to the ReEducation Center. I don't see you on the list for training today."

"I'm not on the list. I am hoping to talk to one of the dissidents. My friend, Katherine Floyd."

He looks down at his data pad, slides his fingers over its surface. I try not to fidget in front of him and pull myself up to my full height. I can almost look him in his eyes.

"She is not scheduled for visitors, Vice Regent."

"I still need to see her."

"This is highly unorthodox, Vice Regent. As you know, she and the other dissidents are going to Mediation this evening. We need to prepare them for exile."

"I won't be long. I just have a few questions for Katherine."

"Vice Regent, I can assure you we have attempted ReEducation procedures to the fullest extent."

"So you're refusing me?"

"Certainly not."

"Good," I say, as I push past him, "set up a room for us. Katherine's not trying to destroy the Kingdom. She's a lost soul in need of ReEducation."

"As I've said, we have attempted every mandated effort to re-educate your...*friend*."

The way he says 'friend' is like he tastes something rancid. I never cared for Warren even when I was a kid. He was in the same training cohort as my father, and they were close, like brothers. As I was growing up, he was often in our pod. He always sat next to me during dinners. His greedy blue eyes, hunting me as I got older. I turned 15 the day before I joined my training cohort. It was the first birthday I would celebrate without my mother. She died the year before on a training exercise in the Outlands. It felt like we'd been mourning her loss since then. My birthday dinner went well. Warren surprised me. His energy felt different. He spent the evening making my father laugh for what seemed like the first time in months and charming Katherine and her mother, Nahla. I remember getting up to go to the bathroom. As I came out of the bathroom, he stepped out of one of a dark corner and placed a cold, clammy hand around my wrist. I yelped and collided with the wall behind me. He chuckled and slid past me into the bathroom. His eyes looked famished, just like now.

"Which door?" I ask, watching his fingers slide across the data pad.

"ReEducation Room One," Warren says, pulling my attention towards the sterile white door in front of us.

"Thank you, Warren."

As I reach for the door knob, I feel the cold wetness of his hand on top of mine. I cringe.

"We'll certainly be watching, Vice Regent," he whispers near my ear.

ReEducation room walls are always light pastel colors. This one has yellow walls. Every teenager spends time in the ReEducation rooms before our service assignments. It's part of our rites of passage. It's an opportunity to relearn, relive, and recommit our lives to the Kingdom. Our mantra must be ingrained in us before we earn our badges of service: Kingdom, Colony, Family. Before The Fall, teenagers were like children. They were monitored and supervised, overscheduled. Their very existence was the practice of avoiding adulthood. In our Kingdom, we are expected to transition to adulthood by age 17. Our world mandates responsibility and order.

I spent most of my adolescence visiting Katherine in these rooms. It's hard to see my best friend like this; her ash brown mane plaited into multiple cornrows; her full lips thin with anger. We were born to be friends. She comes from a founding family; The Prophet is my distant great-grandfather. Our mothers were pregnant at the same time. Our mothers were best friends. But no matter the genetic engineering there is no social engineering that can force two different people to be friends. But it happened. From the moment of our birth, we were inseparable. Katherine makes me laugh and forces me not to take the future and myself too seriously. I often thought that she'd make a much better Vice Regent. Katherine has a brilliant tactician's mind. She's politically motivated and the best debater in our cohort. The problem: she's dangerously rebellious. We spent lots of time sitting across from one another in one of these rooms. Katherine, slouched down in an uncomfortable metal chair with her long legs perched on the table and me, trying to talk some sense into her. But no matter her body language I can tell her mood by her narrow hazel eyes. I try not to avoid their fiery piercing gaze as I tap on the clear table between us. Katherine's virtual file spreads across the glass surface. I highlight the image that reads treason.

"I knew you'd finally come," Katherine says.

"I bet you did. That was some virus in my program."

"Needed a punch to figure it out huh?"

"I suppose."

"So, did you like it?"

"You inserted a virus into my morning Holocise program, Katherine, a virus that could have killed me. Do you think I liked it?"

"It got you here."

"It certainly did."

"I missed you. It's been a month."

I watch Katherine twist a piece of thread from her gray detention issue clothing. Old habits never die.

"You don't have to miss me. You can get out of this."

"It's been a month, Abby."

"You've always been good at getting yourself into messes. You've spent more time in this place getting re-educated than anyone either of us knows. But this is not some prank. This is not tagging murals or scrawling anarchy symbols in permanent ink on your clothes. This is treason. Treason, Katherine."

"Yep, I'm good at getting into trouble. But I've always been better at getting myself out of it. And as much time as I've spent in this fucking basement, I've never done anything that jeopardized our society."

BRIGHT CITY

"Look," I swipe across the glass and flip the digital image of us towards her, "do you remember us six months ago? We were happy we got the commissions we wanted because that meant we'd talk every day. And I knew the only Comm. Officer I'd want in my ear while I was tracking was you. I trusted you, Katherine, and then..."

"And then you thought I betrayed you."

"You did betray me and your family and the Kingdom. But I want to know why."

I watch her stare at the virtual photo. We'd just turned 17. We shared the same tawny brown skin and broad full-lipped smile, but she had that weird asymmetrical haircut with a magenta streak running through her curls. We were thrusting our badges into the camera, arms around each other, huge smiles on our faces. I'd gotten Tracking, and she'd gotten Communications. She was my 'six,' my back when I was out digging for materials beyond our Colony. Then she got arrested.

"You don't want to know why. If you wanted to know why you would have been here a month ago."

"I'm sorry, they have you on the 'no visitors' list." I reach out to touch her hand, but she pulls it away. "You're right. I should've been here as soon as I got back from the DNA collection. I shouldn't have read the list of crimes against you. I just...I'm sorry. I'm here now."

"You picked quite the moment."

"Katherine, look at us," I swipe my finger across the virtual photo enhancing its size. "We both believed in the Kingdom. What changed with you?"

"This girl," she points at the photo, "was beginning to have doubts."

"Doubts about what?"

Katherine stares at me, her hazel eyes clouding with emotion. I resist the urge to push. I can see she's on edge. She could never lie to me.

It's the same look she gave me when we were seven, and she stole my favorite doll. Not because she was mad at me or because she coveted the doll, but because it was my favorite and she wanted to have me with her all the time. Ever since, I could tell her breaking point, the moment when the real truth would spill out of her like a river breaking through a dam.

"Let's start over," I reach into my pocket and push a chocolate-flavored boost bar towards her. It's her favorite treat.

"A bribe." Katherine laughs.

"A token of friendship."

I watch her shoulders ease back as she twirls the lavender wrapper. She looks up at me with a half-smile, the first since I arrived.

"Vice Regent, you have five more minutes with detainee Floyd," Warren's voice announces over the speaker.

"Abby, you are a cog in the system. This utopia, this Kingdom, is just a cloak for the type of fascist societies we studied in history class."

BRIGHT CITY

"Sometimes people need to be led out of their ignorance to get them to conform to peace and equity."

"Exactly my point," Katherine says.

"So you want to end our Kingdom? You want to destroy everything that The Prophet built?"

"The Prophet was nothing more than a CEO of a multinational corporation. The kind that we say destroyed the United States. Why do you and your father and the counsel have monarchal titles? Regent, Vice Regent. Those are just fancy names for CEO, Vice President, CFO, and COO, corporation rule in disguise. Fascism cloaked in utopia, *Vice Regent*."

Katherine's eyes narrow and I know I've lost her.

"Fine, if you won't concede your heretical ramblings, tell me the leader of the rebels, and you can go free."

"Are you serious?"

"Katherine, I spend days and weeks in the Outland. I know the conditions, and I have supplies. You and the others will be sent out there with nothing. Do you understand that?"

"And you call yourselves civilized."

"And you want to destroy us so, call a truce. Tell us who the leader is so you can go free."

I don't expect her to move so quickly. She launches herself over the table and flips me to the floor. I try to fight her off me, but she's always been a few pounds heavier and at least two inches taller.

"Freedom is not cheap, Abigail Drexler. Freedom is the price you pay every day to be able to think and live with dignity. If you think you can bribe me, with some cheap-ass candy bar and use our friendship to manipulate me, then you are going to be a damn good dictator."

An alarm blares and two Retribution soldiers pull Katherine off me then shove her out the door. I pick myself off the floor and adjust my uniform. I look at the picture of us again, our bright smiles, arms around each other, our badges thrust towards the camera. As I shut down her file, I notice the Boost bar smashed into the floor next to my chair. I bend down to scrape it up. A small red data disk pressed into the chocolate.

CHAPTER FIVE

❧ • ❧

I **FLIP THE DATA DISC BETWEEN MY** fingers. I
know I should take this to my dad, but it feels wrong. I
look around my small living pod. I can see every angle
of my tiny room from the foot of my bed. I know I'm alone,
but I feel jittery anyway. For the first time, I am aware that
my pod is full of contraband. Posters of movies from the
1990s tacked to the walls, stacks of DVDs with black-and-
white detective movies from the 1940s haphazardly piled
on a shelf next to the pulp fiction books I salvaged from a
long-destroyed library. I love these things; they have taken
over almost every corner of my pod. The noir and graphic
novels with half-naked women on the peeling covers
spilling out from under my bed, each of them written with
blood and violence and hateful language woven through
their plots. They are my guilty pleasure. I read these pulp
magazines like people consumed "reality" television before
The Fall. Spectacles of hedonism made for the
consumption by the apathetic. Sort of like gladiatorial
games in ancient Greece; blood and mayhem to satiate

tedium. Today, though, I'm utterly aware of the way my pod is different and cluttered. I realize I haven't had an inspection in months. I'm conscious of the attachment I have to this contraband. Each piece challenges our Kingdom's creed of equity and order.

I replay my confrontation with Katherine. This disc is the reason she pinned me to the floor. She was reckless; as usual. I had to pretend I was scraping up the chocolate so the camera wouldn't catch me with the disc. If there's something on it that could compound her guilt, then I don't want to see it. If there's something on it that could save her, then I have no choice. I toss the possibilities over in my mind. I've never seen anything like it before-tiny, red, and razor thin. I insert the disc into an old data drive that I'd found on an expedition and connect it to my viewer. The viewer blinks alive; a picture of 20th century Manhattan skyline backed by a setting sun pixelates into view.

I push copies of tattered and torn graphic novels off the glass table and swipe across the surface below the viewer. When the virtual keyboard blinks alive, I tap, enter. A picture of a large field of daisies floats into the screen. I smile. When I moved into my pod last year, Katherine teased me when I told her I'd named my viewer Daisy. I stand in front of the screen and flick my finger across the picture. The daisies sway as if touched by a breeze.

"Daisy, scan for inconsistencies in the image."

Scanning, the computer states.

I watch the image dissolve and reanimate then dissolve again until the picture enhances a small portion of the field.

"Enlarge," I say.

BRIGHT CITY

Enlarging image

One single daisy fills the viewer. It's pure white with a glistening yellow center as bright as an egg yolk. Two of the petals have red drops on them.

"Analyze image."

Analyzing.

I move closer to the viewer and note I can move the red across the petal so that it nearly coats it.

Decoding urgent message

"Message?"

Message decoded.

"Voice or text?"

Text message playback.

I watch the screen as the words spread across its surface:

Resist genetic assassination through vaccinations and nutritional supplements. Leadership authorizes sterilization for individuals considered unfit to advance Kingdom propaganda. Listen to following voice recording. End.

"Daisy is the voice message on the disc," I ask.

Voice Message available. Decode?

"Decode."

Decoded. Voice message playback: I trust you've inserted Recipe 165 into the nutrition packs of the following colonists: Katherine Floyd, Abram Jamison, and John Calvin. Their genetic lines indicate their strains are weakening. We need to discontinue their fertility.

I step back from the viewer. Genetic Assassination is an abomination. Before The Fall, the former US government, in cooperation with pharmaceutical companies, began to assassinate whole ethnicities of people through genetic tampering in food preservatives. Their machinations created the Dank Plague. The super flu killed millions of people.

"Daisy, analyze voice overlay."

Voice overlay verified.

"Check for inconsistencies in the recording, track for splicing."

Voice overlay verified. No splicing within the recording.

The recording is real. But the voice is hidden by vibrato. Whose voice is it?
"Daisy, separate voice recording from anonymity overlay."

Voice recording overlay separation process starting.

I sit down on my bed as the countdown flashes across the screen. Ten long minutes from now I hope to know what this all means. I hope this can help Katherine. I replay the orders in my head. Genetic assassination. Katherine was so sure that she was righteous in her rebellion against a corrupt society. Somehow she got this information, and now she believes she's a target. Of course, she's angry. She's probably scared out of her mind. But why didn't she come to me? Because she knew I wouldn't believe her. I didn't believe her when I was sitting right in front of her. She's right; she's always been the kid who acted out, who tested boundaries. She challenged instructors. She cut and dyed her hair whenever she wanted, and she regularly retailored her uniform so that the hems were frayed or shorter. But she was a true believer, just like me. She could quote our laws without hesitation. I should have believed she would have a reason to question our society if she found out this information. I still don't think that she would try and physically destroy our Colony.

I walk around my pod. I stuff my pack with my favorite books, Hydro Purifier to make clean water; Thermo sticks for a fire, and Bunk Tent tab for outdoor sleeping. As I'm rolling up my sleeping bag the notification beep at my door makes me jump. I quickly swipe the viewer to hide the countdown then click the bolt on my door.

"Vice Regent, may I have a word," Warren says.

"What do you want?" I ask as he pushes past me into my space without an invitation.

"Packing for the Outlands, I see. Another two-day excursion?" he says, pointing at my nearly full bag and the stacks of equipment next to my bed. I smirk as he tries to lean casually against the wall next to the door.

"Yes, two days towards the South near Minneapolis. I'm revisiting a clan we want to open trade with," I say.

"You will try to be safe, as we could ill afford the death of our Vice Regent," he says.

I cut my eyes at him. A tiny sweat bead speeds down my spine. The room shrinks with his presence.

"Your visit with your *friend* didn't go quite as well as planned."

"It went as well as could be expected," I shrug.

"That's why we have trained ReEducation specialists. Friends and family can be so emotional."

"What can I do for you?" I ask. I quickly glance at my watch, two minutes left for the scan.

"I'd like to discuss your conversation."

"You have the recordings. Go listen to them."

"I'd like to hear what your opinion of your exchange was."

"Why?"

"Just curious. I confess it seems you were able to get your friend to talk more than our specialists could in the month she's been in our care."

"Your *trained* professionals couldn't get anything out of her?" I smirk.

"Touché."

"I'm afraid there's nothing more to report than I'm an

awful friend. She's been in there a month, and I didn't petition to see her sooner. I thought…well the viruses in my morning training program were her idea. She was sending me a message. I just thought…maybe if I went to talk to her, she might tell me who the leader of the dissidents is."

"And you don't think it's her?"

"You think it is," my stomach clenches; at this moment I know it's not her.

"We have some evidence."

"What?"

"Well, of course, I'm not at liberty to say."

"I'll see the evidence at the Mediation tonight."

"But still…I listened to your conversation, and I feel like she was trying to tell you something."

"Why do you say that?"

"I've worked for the ReEducation Center since I was your age. I've been the Director of ReEducation since I was 20. If there is one thing that I know it's that friends who are like family often attempt to use coded language to exchange information."

"I see. And just what do you think Katherine was telling me?"

"You tell me, Vice Regent."

"I'm getting the distinct impression this is turning into an interrogation."

"Well, I am trained to find the truth, Vice Regent."

"Warren, you may be a friend and advisor to my father, but you have no right to question me. Now, I have to finish packing before the Mediation. I'm leaving right after."

A cold smile creases his full lips. His eyes fill with the same hunger from earlier. I shudder.

"Vice Regent, before I go, in history classes they teach about The Dank Plague still?"

"Of course."

"Do they ever talk about its creation?"

"Well, the instructors say that the genetic assassinations came about by mutating the genetic notes in different groups of people. The mutations triggered the disease, which, of course, led to death."

"Yes. Do you know how the scientists did it?"

"Food preservatives are the accepted theory. But of course, you didn't need me to say that. Get to your point so you can get out."

"Yes, food preservatives," Warren moves towards me backing me against the viewer, "but this recipe they found was virtually unstoppable when mixed with certain genetic traits."

"Thanks for the history lesson. You need to leave." I

BRIGHT CITY

sidestep him and move closer to the door.

Voice recognition completed. Information decode finalized. Authenticity verified.

"Guards," Warren yells, a smirk creasing his thick lips.

He turns his back to me as two of the guards from the ReEducation Center grab me and snap plastic restraints on my wrists.

"This is treason! You have no right to detain me!"

"The rest of the history lesson, Vice Regent," he says as he slides his fingers across my Viewer; the field of daisies popping up, "the food preservative weakened certain individuals with specific genetic traits. The government then started mass producing this chemical and flooded the ghettos, boroughs, and other deviant cities with food that used this recipe." My eyes widen when I realize the truth.

"Recipe 165," I whisper.

"So you know of it, Vice Regent."

"You sick asshole."

"Oh," he chuckles, "it's not me, my dear. I am a mere advisor."

I watch as he finishes typing and the computer reveals the single red-tipped daisy. The countdown ends.

"Computer, security code 827. Computer complete verification and open all files," Warren says.

Security code acknowledged.

The viewer fills with blueprints of the five colonies in the Kingdom and all the weak spots in their mainframes. I could see several red X's across them most likely indicating where the group had already infiltrated.

"Verify," Warren says as he turns towards me.

Subject: Dr. Richard Drexler, Ambassador of Drexton Colony One and Regent of Drexler Kingdom.

My eyes widen. My father? My father ordered this? I shake my head and tears burn the corners of my eyes. It can't be. He'd never do something like this.

"Sometimes, genetic lines weaken over time," Warren says as he slips a black sack over my head.

CHAPTER SIX

ॐ•ॐ

W E HUSTLE INTO THE PIT OF THE Mediation chamber. Colonists fill the stadium-style seats rising above our wooden benches. Mediation attendance isn't mandatory for colonists. But today they all want to see the Regent's daughter exiled for treason. I look up at the large elevated mahogany desk on the platform above us. I try to make eye contact with my father. But he stares straight ahead. I feel small. Members of the Mediation Councils from the other colonies flicker into focus on the giant screens lining the walls. Our cousins from the South are darker than we are in the north. They have more defined cheekbones and narrower eyes. They speak with strange accents that twang, combine sounds that roll "R's," and take significant pauses in between words. The notice bell chimes three times and silence settles over the colonists. No one looks at us.

"Our Kingdom is over 100 years old; we have stood against The Fall. We have survived The Dank Plague. We have prospered because we followed The Prophet's teaching to the letter. In one of his many proclamations, he talked about rebellion. He said that in any utopian society, even in the best utopian societies, there would be individuals who will rebel against perfection. He cautioned ReEducation as a first response. But he believed that we exile those who did not submit to ReEducation so as not to taint the rest of the community. In the past, we have removed only a few of our colonists. Those few who rebel walk out the gates without much fuss, content to remove themselves from perfection and into oblivion. They prefer to live in a world where every day is a struggle against the elements and the descendants of those who created The Fall. But rarely are we challenged by such malicious behavior by one of our own. Rarely do we, as a Colony, as a Kingdom, stand before one another and call one of our own a traitor. Today is the saddest day when children of key families in our great society attempt to destroy our way of life."

I frown at Warren's smarmy pontificating and turn to try to catch my father's attention. Even from the lower bench, I can see his eyes are tired. I note that Counsel Nahla Floyd, Katherine's mother, pats his hand when Warren points at the four of us.

"What are the charges?" Counsel Floyd asks.

I notice smile play across Warren's lips just before he begins reading from the virtual files.

"One count each, willful destruction of Kingdom property, intent to incite mass hysteria, slander, libel of the sitting Regent, intent to dismantle critical systems in the security of our Colony, and, of course, treason."

"What is the proof?" asks Counsel Magnus who sits to my father's left.

BRIGHT CITY

Warren manipulates the glass panel on his podium, and a holographic image rises above the crowd. He flicks and flips the plans outlining a long and systematic strategy that at its end goal was to destroy the primary energy routers which connect the colonies to the complicated satellite system we use for communication and survival. Each holographic image is more damning than the next. The whispers amongst the colonists rise with each revelation. I'm startled by the details of the plans beyond the destruction of the satellite system. There are plans to murder the Council members and the sitting Vice Regents in the other colonies. Finally, after several slides that show how they were going to destroy critical food systems, the collection houses in the Outlands, and the incineration lists of genetic material;, an image of my father with a large red X over his face appears. I glance at Katherine, John, and Abram. They don't look particularly surprised by the detailed description of our alleged plans.

"You were going to kill us. You were going to kill my father!" I whisper to Katherine.

"And now, according to Warren, you were too," she replies. I feel her fingertips snake around my own. She gives me a warm smile. I can see apologies in her eyes. Part of me wants to wrap my arms around her and tell her that we'll be ok. Part of me wants to smack her around. I don't want to believe she would go this far.

When the hologram disintegrates, the chatter in the room dies.

"Where did you find this information?" my father asks, breaking the silence in the chamber.

"Regent Drexler, I regret to inform you and the council that I found it in the Vice Regent's chambers," Warren says.

"Why were you searching the Vice Regents pod," Counsel Floyd asks.

"The Vice Regent made an unauthorized visit to one of the dissidents this afternoon. They got into what seemed like a staged physical confrontation. I suspected that information passed between the two of them."

"And on whose authority?" Counsel Magnus asks.

"Why of course," Warren says as he turns to face me, "Regent Richard Drexler."

The mediation chamber explodes with chatter and calls for exile. I shake my head and look desperately at the dais. My father looks down at me. His almond shaped eyes are distant and lack emotion. I feel tears threaten the corner of my eyes. How could he believe I would destroy the Kingdom? That I would ever want to kill him?

In the days before The Fall, people would have lawyers represent them. There'd often be days before the trials would be over. Mounds of paperwork to sift through, testimonies to compile, reviewing evidence and refuting statements. But in our Kingdom, ReEducation is the process intended to reconcile the guilty into the community. If ReEducation doesn't work then exile is the only way. No trial, public exile; which means death.

"Before I sentence you to exile," my father says as the chamber quiets down to hushed whispers, "I would ask each of you to come forward and name the leader of your rebellion. If you do, you will be remanded to the ReEducation center for no less than six months and sent to live Above tending to the elderly, but we will spare you."

For a moment, it seems as if the chamber is holding its collective breath. Then Katherine steps forward. Then John, the young man to her right. Then Abram, the young man to her left.

"I am the leader," the trio says in unison.

"Impossible," my father says with a sigh.

I can feel the room watching Katherine. She nods at the boys who both take one step back.

"I would like to speak," Katherine says.

"Are you going to tell us who pushed you into this rebellion?" my father asks.

"What kind of society exiles its people to certain death because they question the motives of its leaders?"

"We are not leaving you to die. You are choosing this," my father says.
"Wait," I stand up and move next to Katherine, "aren't you going to ask why they tried to destroy the Kingdom?"

"Why you tried to destroy the Kingdom," Warren corrects.

"I am not a traitor," I growl.

"Abigail, you were told not to go to the ReEducation

center today, and you disobeyed my orders…"

"I defied you to go see my friend. My friend, Daddy. My friend!"

"Do not interrupt me again, young lady!"

The chamber goes silent. My father's lips smash to a firm line. I feel Katherine's body stop me from stepping back.

"You are complicit in whatever is happening here. Why are you trying to destroy the Kingdom?"

"I'm not. And I don't think they are either."

"So you're calling the Regent a liar," Warren shouts.

The chamber explodes with cries of treason and demands for our exile. Beneath the yelling, I can even hear a few voices calling for our death. I glare at Warren. His face looks predatory.

"You disobeyed me by going to see Katherine. Why didn't you tell me about the glitches in your exercise program?"

"Viruses happen all the time," I say, moving closer to the dais, "I didn't think they meant anything."

"Abigail," my father, says rising from his seat, "I need you, to be honest, or you will follow your friends into exile. Why are you trying to destroy the Kingdom?"

"Dad, I promise I'm not, and I don't think they are either."

BRIGHT CITY

He sits, the Mediation chamber is silent. A frown deepens the corners of his mouth.

"It is evident to me that the four of you are committed to this treason," my father says.

"No," I say.

"If you want me and this counsel to believe you tell us who is the leader of your rebellion," my father demands.

"I think this rebellion has to do with recipe 165," I reply.

"Abigail, who is the leader of your rebellion?"

"Your voice is on a recording ordering the genetic assassination of their families," I yell.

The Retribution soldiers who were with Warren in my pod grab me. They shove me into my seat. Katherine pats my hand. I don't look at her; I'm afraid I might break down.

"You and your co-conspirators stand before the Colony in this chamber and accuse me of an abomination against the Kingdom," my father yells as he rises from his seat, "You will tell me who the leader of your rebellion is and you will say it now!"

"You are the leader of this rebellion," Katherine shouts.

"Excuse me?"

"Your actions against colonists make you the leader of

the rebellion. And understand this, Regent Drexler, you may exile us but one day we will come back, and when we do we will bring proof of a better world."

"You won't be coming back. I can assure you," Warren shouts.

"Murderer!" Katherine shouts back.

"You see," Warren yells, "We will not tolerate your terroristic fear mongering in the Kingdom. By the power of the sitting Regent, you are hereby exiled!"

The Retribution soldiers grab us and begin elbowing us through the crowd.

I hear my father's voice rise above the colonists. At first, I can't understand what he's saying. But then his words begin to fill the mouths of the colonists around us. Katherine looks back at me. The anger in her hazel eyes burns against my terror. I've been to the Outlands but never without supplies. She gives me a wicked smile before black sacks cover our heads. As we are pushed out the doors, I hear the rhythmic and hypnotic chant of our society motto "Kingdom, Colony, Family," "Kingdom, Colony, Family" flood the chamber.

CHAPTER SEVEN

❧ • ☙

I'VE BEEN COUNTING THE DAYS ON the road away from the Colony from a tiny cell on a large dark bus trekking through the Outlands. The cells are sealed most of the day. We use the toilet twice. We have room to stand up, and there's a padded bench to sit and sleep. I've counted four days. Four days ago I was Vice Regent of the Drexton Kingdom. I lived in Colony One. I've never been this far away from the Colony. My longest Tracking mission was two days at the most. Our instructors teach us that diseases, sewage, and waste contaminate the outer lands. Through a small window, as we bump across dented and rarely used roads, I see this was a lie. The landscape is rugged, but some places are lush; filled with long grass and wild herds of Buffalo. We pass houses and storefronts nearly swallowed by twisting ivy and vegetation, humanity's creations devoured by nature. The Outlanders, which pass by our bus, are not deformed or ill. Some are stout; windburned and sunburned but look healthy. Instinctively, I long for my kit to take samples.

I've had time to think about the evidence presented from the Mediation chamber. I turn my father's attitude over and over in my head. Why wouldn't he listen to my side? Why listen to Warren instead of me? It's true that they are like family; like Katherine and me. But I doubted Katherine when she needed me. I think about the red disc, the information on it. I looked guilty. Katherine and the guys looked guilty. I can't prove it, but I think Warren is behind this. But why he wanted me exiled is a mystery. I'm certain if he is behind this, and he used Katherine to get to me. But why get rid of me? Why steal the sitting Regent's child; from him, his friend? And even if my father's intentions were to protect the Kingdom; why wouldn't he have put me in ReEducation to find out more? Why exile me immediately?

My father is a true believer. He raised me to be a true believer. Did his faith get shaken because he thought I was a traitor? I hug myself; squeezing into a ball on the narrow bench. I think back to when I was nine. My father had taken me to one of the towers on the wall. The Retribution soldiers spend their time on the wall watching and protecting it. It was the first time that I'd been from underground. He held me in his arms, looking dapper in his black uniform. Back then, my mother dressed me in miniature copies of his uniform. Her twins, she'd coo. I remember loving the feel of the wind against my face. He held me so that I faced the Outlands.

"You rule this land. Our family rules this land," he'd said.

"I don't know what rule means," I'd said.

"It means that everywhere you look, it is yours. Like your doll," he'd said, handing me my stuffed rag doll, "She belongs to you; all of this belongs to you."

BRIGHT CITY

"Mine?"

"Yours, but…"

"But what Daddy?"

"You can't ever betray it or our family. Do you know what that means?"

"No," I'd said, hugging my doll.

"It means telling lies."

"No lies, Daddy, that's bad."

"Yes, that's bad. The people before, they told lies. They made out there a scary place."

"I'm not scared."

"I know because you are brave."

"Like you!"

"Yes, like me."

"Can we go out there, Daddy?"

"When you're older, you'll explore this whole world. And only if you eat your vegetables and you follow the rules, and you follow the teachings of The Prophet."

"I will!"

Suddenly, the bus jerks to a stop. I wipe the tears from my eyes and look out of the tiny gated window. I see green mossy fields bumping up against burned out brick and steel buildings. I hear muffled noises beyond my cell door. Five minutes later there's a dull pop. After ten minutes a Retribution soldier opens my cell door and slides a black hood over my face.

I stumble between the two bulky Retribution soldiers. My legs seize and ache from inactivity. I feel a knife slice through the binding on my wrists. I blink against the flash of light whooshing into my eyes when the hood is snatched off. I rub my eyes to get them to focus.

"You probably don't want to move any further," says one of the soldiers.

I take my hands from my eyes. I stumble away from the edge of a large crater.

"Why are we here?" I ask.

"The end of the road, Vice Regent," says the other soldier.

"Where are the other exiles? Which direction should I go?"

"You'll find the exiles in the pit."

I am confused. I don't see any tents or signs of life; just mounds of gravel here and there. Then I look closer and see a peek of gray from between clumps of reddish-colored mud. I follow it up to the brown arm it barely covers. I see Katherine's face, contorted, eternally caught in mid fear. I realize then that exile means murder. Scattered in the basin are decaying bodies. Human bodies. Heat fills my chest as tears burn the corners of my eyes. I collapse to my knees perilously close to the side of the ditch. Sobs heave from my throat. I can barely breathe. My best friend, murdered over lies. I hear the familiar click of a 9mm. I pull myself off my knees. If I'm going to die; I'll do it standing up.

"Any last words," chuckles one of the soldiers.

I shake my head. Then silence.

From an early age, we train in combat techniques. Knowing that the end of the world was coming, The Prophet combined education with military training. Everyone had to learn the basics. Trackers spend days or weeks in the Outlands. Sometimes we interact with hostile Outlanders. So we train with the Retribution soldiers. They apparently forgot that fact.

I drop to the ground. I catch the soldier's off guard and kick the nearest soldier's legs out from under him. I hear his gun explode. The other soldier, blond hair peeking out from under his cap, drops his weapon, blood trickles between his fingers as he grips his bicep. I punch the closest soldier between his legs and snatch his gun before it hits the ground. I stand up on the lip of the pit and point the weapon in their direction.

"We have ourselves a standoff, fellas," I say, quoting a favorite western movie from my contraband DVD collection.

"We have orders, Vice Regent." One of the soldiers, the bleeding one says.

"You're not going to kill me. You know that right?"

"Nobody said to kill you," says the other soldier as he

struggles to his feet.

"You just tried to kill me, asshole."

"We were just joking, but we do have orders," the bleeding one says.

"What orders?"

"You are a traitor. We saw your plans at Mediation."

"You also heard me say my father ordered the genetic assassination of children and families."

"You're a traitor. You'd say anything to implicate the Regent," says the wounded soldier.

"Yeah, what we saw were plans for the dissidents to destroy the Kingdom," the other soldier agrees.

"Implicate the Regent? I am his daughter! I wouldn't lie about my father. I need to find out if what is on that disc is the truth. I'm not a traitor, and neither were the people you killed. So, you have two options. You can let me go and tell my father that you did your job, or you can stay here and die," I click the gun.

I hear the roar of engines only seconds before a rifle blast explodes the wounded soldier's blonde head. I hit the dirt. The other guard scrambles to the dead man's gun. He crawls towards me, and a band of men encircles us. Their bikes block every escape route except into the pit. I am not going in there. I stand with the gun at my side.

"What do we have here?" says a fat man to my left.

BRIGHT CITY

"We were uh...out here searching for some of our people," I lie.

"You can put the gun down. You're surrounded," the fat man continues.

"You just killed one of my guards. Why would I put my gun down?"

"We must be mistaken, little lady. 'Cause we thought they was trying to kill you," says a grungy boy who looks about my age.

"Well, you were mistaken. Now we need to get back on the road."

"This was not the deal, assholes," yells the soldier at my feet.

"Deal," I ask.

"Looks like you were going to break the deal," the fat man says pulling the soldier onto his feet by his neck. The soldier winces as the big man squeezes a bit then shoves him back.

"What deal?" I demand.

"Ah, little lady, it's not for me to say but someone important is looking forward to meeting you."

"Hey man, you killed my comrade! That's gonna cost you," the soldier yells.

"Well, then let me pay my debt."

A warm splatter of blood hits my face as the soldier crumbles next to me. A whoop comes from my left. The fat man raises his gun. The band of men surrounding us laughs and cheers.

"Who brokered this deal?" I demand "What's your clan name? I don't see any tattoos. Who's your leader?"

They look at each other for a moment then laugh some more. The group smells so bad it makes my stomach turn. I look past the furthest man and see that no one seems to have noticed the truck. If I can get to it, I can put some distance between these assholes and me.

"Why don't we...uh...take you to our leader," the fat man chuckles as he moves towards me.

His hand clamps my shoulder. I shove my left elbow into his chest. When he bends over, I bring up my elbow under his chin. Three black teeth spill to the ground. I twist away from him and sprint towards the truck. I shoot one of the men in front of me, hitting him in the shoulder. Mid-stride, the fat man, snatches my legs from under me. I slam into the ground. The gun flies ahead of me.

"Now girly, let's see if you can get me off of you."

I thrust my head back. I hear his nose crack. I try to slither from beneath him. I get a few feet and feel him pull me up by my braids. He twists me towards him. His hot breath smells like rotten meat and alcohol. Around us, the men yell, whistle and clap as the fat man backhands my cheek. He slams me onto the dusty ground. I land on my back. I taste iron at the corner of my mouth. The fat man grabs my right arm. Pain shoots down my right side. I reach back and grab a small stone. I clock him in the head. He stumbles back as I scramble backward. He charges me. Blood streams down his bald head. I spit a bloody glob in his face. I try to struggle to my feet. He picks me up and smashes me stomach first to the ground. His large hands rip the back of my pants. I feel the chilling wind against my lower back.

"I'll teach you to spit on me, you little bitch," the fat man growls.

At this moment, I hear my heart thump. The catcalls and whooping fade against the thwack of an unfurling zipper. The man's rough hands scrape across my exposed butt. He yells to the men to hold my legs. I try desperately to squirm away.

Thump. Thump.

Hands release my legs. I scramble the last few inches to the gun. Large boot steps on it. A scream breaks the silence. I realize I'm the one screaming.

"Ok, assholes, our *leader*, is gonna want to meet this young lady," a husky voice shouts above the men.

The sound of the cycles roaring to life splits the air. I feel the cold breath of someone near my ear.

"It's ok. You're safe."

Against my will, I pass out.

CHAPTER EIGHT

❧ • ❧

"Wake up."

The soft distinctly male voice clashes with my throbbing headache. My body aches; my muscles burn. I struggle to open my eyes. I look around a drafty dimly lit room. Sunlight peeks from beneath the cracks of the small tent. I see a body standing in the shadows.

"Get away from me," I scream.

The young man jumps into a crease of light. Some contents from a medium-sized wooden bowl slosh down the front of his shirt. He runs a hand through his tightly shaved black curls then swipes at the drops of liquid.

"Calm down, Abigail," he says.

"Where am I? Who are you? How do you know my name?"

"I'm Cleary. You're in Knute. You're safe. Here, I brought you something for your stomach."

He shoves the bowl under my nose. I look down at my clothing. The scratchy material of the khaki-colored shirt and pants feels alien against my skin. I bring my hands up against my throbbing cheek. I touch the area gently. I wince, and so does Cleary.

"You're a bit banged up," he says.

"Yeah, I hope I get to meet that asshole again," I reply flexing my stiff fingers.

"I don't think he hopes to meet you again," he chuckles.

I reach for the bowl. The clear broth smells spicy and sweet.

"Spoon?"

"Sorry, you'll have to just," he says, mimicking putting an imaginary bowl to his mouth.

"Yeah, drink out of the bowl," I say, rolling my eyes.

The broth is warm. The sweet-tasting spice feels good against my raw throat. My stomach growls with delight. I scoot back and cross my legs under me. I drink and think about my father. His betrayal. He believes I'm a traitor, and I know he's one. He had my best friend killed. He ordered the murder of colonists. I have to find out the truth. But first I have to get away from these savages.

"How long was I out?"

"About a week."

"Excuse me?"

"You were out for a week. My dad was worried the whole fight might've killed you but the Medicine Merchant told us you were fine. That's the last of the meds," he said pointing at the bowl.

I look at the soup then back at him. He smiles and shrugs. I notice a brief glint of sun dance off his bright hazel eyes. They remind me of Katherine's. I take another sip of soup; I try not to cry.

"It's ok," he says, mimicking drinking again.

I frown but sip the broth slower. Cleary paces the green tent checking the front flap periodically. The floor of the tent is sand, but the tent itself looks sturdy. Someone stenciled the word ARMY across the tops of the walls. A cot, a wooden chair against a small desk and a table with an old flame lamp decorate the sparsely furnished tent. I finish the broth and set the bowl on the table. I feel less achy but still stiff. I uncurl my legs; a burning raw pain creeps through my upper thighs. The memory of the fat man's hands on my body flood my mind.

"So, your…friends…they tried to rape me...did they manage to…"

"What? No, hell, no," he says.

"You said that way too quickly."

"They didn't."

"Yeah, I don't know you so…"

"I'm the clan leader's son. I forbid that kind of behavior and my father would too."

"Thanks," I sigh.

I have no reason to believe him. But I hope for now that it's true.

"I got these other clothes for you," he says, pointing towards a brown satchel, lying on the ground, "I gotta take you to meet my father."

"I don't think I'm up for socializing," I murmur.

"So there's the clothes. I'm gonna step out and then," Cleary sheepishly holds up two white strips, "I gotta cuff you."

"No way that's going to happen," I say.

"Listen, I have to. I don't want to, but I have to. Just please make this easy a'ight?

Now I'm gonna step out, you get dressed, and we'll go to the meeting."

"Hold on. I just woke up. I'm just supposed to follow you out of here?"

"You have to."

"No, I don't."

"Listen, you don't have a choice. Get dressed."

"Not until you tell me more information."

"Look, you have no reason to trust me. I get it. If I was going to do anything to you, I could have."

"Yeah, that makes me trust you even more."

"My god! Look I promise I won't let anything happen to you. Now get dressed!"

I dig through the bag: underwear, pants, boots, and a black t-shirt. I slip on the clothes. They are softer than the clothes I woke up in from repeated washing. I check for an alternative exit. I don't want to be a captive. I have to find a way out of here, but first I have to find transportation. There's no telling how long it took to get here or how far it is from the colony.

"So," I shout through the flap, "did you see that bus at the pit?"

"Yep," he says.

"Is it here?"

"Why would you want to know that?"

"Well, maybe you could take me back there so I can start it up. You can have that in exchange for my freedom."

"I figured it out. Don't worry about it. Now hurry up, we have a meeting to go to."

The pants are a bit baggy, but the shoes fit perfectly. And by the time I slip the t-shirt over my head, I feel safer and more confident. I smile at the possibility that I can get to the bus. If I can escape, I can put some welcome distance between this town and me. I take a breath and pick up the wooden bowl.

"Hey, do you have a belt for these pants?" I call out.

"Oh sorry, you can have mine I…"

Taking the bait Cleary comes through the flap headfirst. I hit him across the face with the wooden bowl. Then I kick him out of the way of the flap. He stumbles and crashes across the room with an oomph. I sprint out of the tent and take a quick right.

"You don't know where the hell you're going Abby," I say aloud.

Ahead, I hear clanking and smell burning iron. I see a semi-smashed car peeking over a crumbling wall. Excited, I know I can hide in a car until I can sneak out after dark. I skid to a halt in the open area. Piles and piles of rusted cars and other machines line the rows; crookedly stacked one on top of the other. It is a maze of dead technology.

"Abigail!" I hear Cleary yell behind me.

I dash towards the first narrow opening amongst the piles. I run through aisles deftly avoiding jagged edges and low-lying frames jut out. Finally, I burst out from a row close to a dimly lit shack. Through the large windowless hole, I can see the bus. I run straight for the door. I can hear Cleary's thudding boots behind me. I throw open the door and run headlong into a massive body. I fall flat on my butt.

"Well, hello there Abigail."

Rubbing my forehead, I look up just as I hear a breathless Cleary skid to a halt behind me.

"Hey Dad," Cleary says.

The small table in front of me groans with red meats, sweet smelling stews, and grilled vegetables. My stomach growls. I stare at my empty plate willing my stomach to shut up. I gently pull at the white plastic band securing my left wrist to the arm of a wooden chair and check out the room. Cleary's dad, Saul, had his guards bring me to his house at the edge of the small town.

"You're hungry," Pamela, Cleary's sister, says, pushing a piece of meat onto my plate from the passing tray.

"I'm not eating."

"You have to. You need your strength."

I scowl at my plate as she fills it with vegetables and meat covered in deep brown gravy. I pull at the band keeping me tied to the chair then scoot away from the food.

"I'll eat when I'm free," I say.

She nods with a polite smile rising to her strange nearly-white blue eyes. She's a survivor of the Dank Plague. The eyes, the white blond hair stark against her coffee-colored skin. They are signifiers that her mother had it and passed it on to her in utero. I glance across the table at Cleary and catch his scowl. I can see the bruise across his cheek darkening his brown skin.

"Eat," Saul says, jabbing his fork at my plate.

"I don't know if you've seen your fat henchman today or your son's face but let's just say I can be very deadly."

Saul laughs, spoons some mashed substance onto my plate and shoves a spoon in my free hand.

"I bet you'll try."

"Let me go."

"No. Now eat before I have Ivan, or as you call him, 'the fat man' come force you to eat."

Ivan leans against the front door. His face is a mishmash of bruises and bandages. I smirk and straighten up in my chair. I think about Katherine and my father. He would have a disapproving frown on his face if he saw me acting like a spoiled child. Katherine would tell me to cut the shit and eat. She'd push me to survive by any means necessary. These Outlanders may have me now but that doesn't mean they'll have me forever and the first thing I need to do is get stronger and then make a plan. It was stupid for me to think I could get away without any supplies. Besides, what would happen if I showed up back at the Colony? I need more information about this place, the land surrounding it, and the distance between here and the Colony. To do all that, I have to play along. I have to shove down my pride. I sigh then cram some food in my mouth. My stomach gurgles its approval.

"That's better. Now, tell me, what you were doing near the pit."

"I already told you."

"No, I want to know why your Colony tried to kill you when we had a deal."

Before dinner, Saul explained the agreement. He'd gotten a letter from a leader in our Colony regarding a trade. The Colony would exchange citizens for legitimate samples of Recipe 165. Saul said the deal had been going on for years. He'd just simply traffic the citizens to one of the Outlander clans, but he wondered why I was different. Why did they want to kill me rather than honor their deal? I tried to explain that I didn't know anything about a deal or why they would want me dead rather than alive.

"I can't tell you anything else."

"You think I'm a fool, don't you?"

Saul pushes close to my face. I can see a spark in his bright blue eyes.

"No, I don't."

"You think I don't know after all these years about your little underground hovel where you *moles* crawl out and dispose of your castoffs. We've watched your people for years. We've watched as you've passed out treats to the poor saps that surround your walled city. We've dug those godforsaken tags out the skin of people who go by your dirty walls," Saul says.

"I don't know what you're talking about."

"Oh, I know you do, *Abigail Drexler*."

Saul leans away from me his crooked-toothed smile caressing his lips.

"Well, if you know who I am then you know what we can do to your little town."

"The letter was right. You will make a hell of a trade," Saul says as raises his glass in my direction with a laugh that chills me.

He turns his attention to the men passing through the house and makes a weirdly crass joke.

I can barely breathe. Trade?

"My dad is not a mean man. You know that right? We are not mean people," Pamela whispers below Saul's raucous laughter.

"This seems pretty fucking lousy," I say, twisting my cuffed wrist.

"He may be misguided, but he is the leader of our people. He made a deal for our clan."

"Then, whoever he made this bargained with screwed him cause I'm not gonna just be held captive. Your dad just made the worst deal of his life."

The days since I have arrived in Knute have passed surprisingly quickly. When I've had free time, I've explored every inch of this place, looking and hoping for a way to escape. The town itself seems to be oval-shaped with only one way to exit or enter. The junkyard is near the front with its rickety-looking towering piles of smashed cars and metal guarding both sides of the large archway. A wooden fence surrounds the town with crawly barbed wire weaving across the tops of the sharp wooden stakes. I'm Pamela's shadow. She has three girls who take care of her clothing, bedroom and most of her meals. We spend time in the infirmary where she stops at every bed offering a kind word. We often meet with the townswomen who cook together over the communal fire pit outside of the longhouse, which sits at the center of the town. She teaches me how to cook on an actual fire, clean game animals and harvest food in her private garden. When we sit with the women after they've fed their families, we never eat. She doesn't think it's proper. She is the clan leader's daughter, and she has her food. She wears this distinction as an honor.

Tonight, we are sitting with the women, listening to the latest gossip about the men. We hear a scream from the marketplace. Forgetting myself, I run towards the sound. I pounce on the back of the muscular man standing over a bruised, russet-colored young woman, punching the back of his head. He flips me off him then leans back in to smack the teenager on her already swollen cheek. Desperately, I look around for a weapon. I crack him over his back with a small bolt of fabric. He turns on me.

"I'm just gonna say this once; don't do this," I say.

"This is a slave," he growls, "and you are lucky that you are Pamela's pet or you'd be headed where she is."

"Slave?"

I look at the young woman and notice the shackles on her ankles.

"I don't believe in slaves. That's old world."

"Look around *you mole*; this *is* the old world," he

snarls, turning towards the young woman and snatching her up by her wrists.

"I'm not gonna let you take her," I say.

"You can't fucking stop me," he says.

"Carl, please," Pamela says, coming from behind me her hand on my back, "she doesn't understand."

"You make her understand," he sneers through sun-cracked lips.

"Yo, Carl, hand the girl over," Cleary says, appearing from behind a crowd that's formed around us.

"She's mine, Cleary, mine! I won her fair and square!"

"Yeah, yeah, I know Carl, listen, I'll trade you. I got some equipment that I think will work for your cycle, and I'll negotiate a two-day pass into Minneapolis. You know the type of women they have there. This one, she's nowhere near worth that."

The man looks between the three of us. I shift the bolt that's gotten heavy in my hand.

"Deal," he says, spitting in his palm and gripping Cleary's hand.

The crowd disperses as the man drops the girl to the ground and walks off with Cleary towards the junkyard. Cleary looks over his shoulder, frowning in my direction.

"Come on precious," Pamela says, pulling the girl up from the ground, "let's get you to the infirmary."

Some of the women who followed us over to the marketplace put their arms around the girl and lead her towards the large white tent adjacent to the longhouse.

"Slaves?" I say, turning towards Pamela.

"Some people have to sell themselves into servitude," she says, as we walk behind the women.

"This is barbaric," I say, shaking my head.

"You've lived a life of privilege."

"You've got some nerve," I scoff.

"No, I know that I have privilege, I know that if it wasn't for my father, I'd be a servant or a slave or something much worse, something I hope you don't see while you're here."

"What could be worse than being forced to serve someone against your will?"

"I hope you never find out, but you judge us. You judge my father even though he's given you to me. And I've taken care of you."

"What?"

"Yes, you belong to me, for now. But I would never treat you as if you belong to me. I recognize who I am; my leadership to these women means everything. I am their leader, and I don't pretend that I'm not. That's the difference between you and me."

BRIGHT CITY

"You're no better than him."

She smiles. I want to smash her face.

"No, I suppose to you, I am beneath you, just like him. But to the women we spend time with, you are beneath me. All this 'equality' that you bore me with does not exist out here. And you would be wise to understand that," she says, turning her back on me.

I slump to the ground outside the infirmary and cry for the first time in weeks. The weight of the truth crushes my bravado. I am well and truly screwed.

CHAPTER NINE

દે•ન્ક

THERE IS A RHYTHM TO LIFE IN Knute that I've started to accept. Men go out on raiding parties once a week. Pamela and I sit with the other women, listen to gossip and take care of her garden. The marketplace is bustling most days with traders coming in and out. Pamela greets the clan leaders, plays with their children and negotiates with their women for spices or fabric. Cleary keeps his distance from us. I've been around him a few times in the infirmary when he brings in a young woman he's managed to rescue from the raiding parties. Saul keeps insisting that he's going to trade me, though Pamela promises he won't. I can hear them sometimes arguing, her soft but stern voice against his booming one. She's won so far.

Pamela hasn't mentioned our disagreement again, but it weighs on me. I dwell on it as I work alongside her and eat with her and her family. I tell myself that I am the Vice Regent. But am I? I feel myself blending into this life, being kept like a pet, at Pamela's beck and call like her handmaidens. Being at her disposal, it makes me think a lot about the Colony. I am beginning to see the pedestal I occupied, the privileges I took for granted. I think back on my childhood and remember that from a very young age people treated me differently. I knew I was going to be a leader and even if I didn't always believe in the doctrine of our Kingdom, I upheld it above everything, including my friendship with Katherine. Now I see how she tried to talk to me so many times. So many times she tried to get me to come down off my pedestal and realize our society was smothering so many of the Colonists. But I refused. I refused because I didn't want to hear her. I was just like the people from before The Fall; I passed out crumbs while I ate cake. Oh certainly, the Kingdom was safer and more equitable than the societies before The Fall. The Kingdom was certainly more safe and fair than Knute, but we were blind to how far we had gotten away from the utopia my many time's great grandfather imagined. In Knute, everyone knows and seems to accept their place. There is no class mobility.

Accepting this cannot be an option for me. And yet, I find myself going along with it. Finding myself being silent when I should speak up. I've stood with Pamela in the slave markets and watching the men sell women. I've watched the working men berated and beaten into working harder and faster. I've watched and forced myself not to turn my head away. I will not forget these moments. And when I return to my home in the Kingdom, I will tell the people about these things I've seen and experienced. I will not let these things just die in my mind for the safety of those walls. No one in those walls is safe as long as this exists outside of them. No one is safe as long as banishment to this exists.

"We have to oversee the deliveries this morning,"

Pamela says as I adjust the shoulders of her shirt.

"I figured. You're wearing your working gear," I say, as Pamela slips on her boots.

"The Cycle is happening in a few weeks, and we have to get ready," she says as she slides a small dagger into a holster on her belt.

"The Cycle?"

"Twice a year the clan leaders come together to trade and settle disputes. My father hosts every year."

"How many more clans are there?"

"Many more. You have been in that hole for far too long. You'll get to see how big the world is. For all the technological advancements you boast about your world seems tiny."

As I follow Pamela to the marketplace, I think about how little I know about the Outlands. She's right my society is very technologically advanced. And I know about at least three clans. They're small. And the numbers in their group's shift often. They never seemed very organized. But I didn't even know about this town. And now I know that my father has known about it for a very long time. Why would he keep something like this from us? I doubt any of us would want to join this type of life: outhouses, slavery and barely any running water. Our Colony is clean, healthy and sustainable. I think about Saul's words that they've been watching our Colony. We'd be able to protect the Colony from a siege. Why not make these people our allies and trade with them openly? Is this what Katherine found out? Did she discover we were selling human beings for Recipe

165? That seems pretty obvious now, but why would my father do this?

The noise in the marketplace is like a well-oiled machine. The shouting, laughter, friendly bickering and haggling hums around us as Pamela supervises her father's men while they unload their trucks. After unloading, she gives each man a stack of wooden trading chips. The chips are the currency for the marketplace, the casino, or the whorehouse. I follow behind her with her satchel of toys and sweets for the children in the hospital as she talks with one of the women who supervises the food for the Cycle. I half listen to their chattering. Pamela is an excellent leader. My father would be proud of her. She is the leader he always wanted me to be. Good with the people, kind but disciplined with her boundaries. Before we can make it to the door, a young woman runs out of the hospital towards us.

"Miss, miss, something is happening with my son, Kyrie," the woman says almost tripping in front of Pamela.

"What is it, Miriam?"

"I brought him in this morning. But he's burning up. Nothing has helped. He can't keep anything down."

Pamela takes off, and I run after her. We follow Miriam to the end of the long room and stop by the small bed with netting around it. There are two long houses in the compound. One for large communal gatherings and the other is the hospital. They are both built with logs and pitch and remind me of the structures I'd seen when we studied ancient cultures. Two large stoves in the middle of the walkways heat the hospital. The communal log house has a massive fireplace at one end. The hospital has at least 50 slender twin-size beds along the walls with plenty of sunshine filling the expansive space through the multiple windows and the skylight in the roof. The beds are mostly empty. A broken arm here, a dog bite there, a few people cordoned off with the flu. But when we approach Kyrie's bed I know exactly how bad the situation is. Flushed tawny skin, sweating through his clothes, and red infection lines crawling up his arms while his fingertips and lips are turning blue.

"Kyrie, where did you go, what did you do!" I yell, shaking him awake.

"Nowhere."

"This is no time to lie kid."

He turns his head to face his mother. She's a wreck. Crying and shaking in Pamela's arms.

"Talk to her Kyrie," Pamela urges.

"I was down by the patch. Where we go to practice hunting."

"The patch?" I ask.

"Yara, go find Cleary," Pamela shouts. A young woman dressed in white runs out the door.

"You don't know where the patch is," I ask Pamela.

She ignores me and shushes Miriam, motioning for another worker to lay her in the bed next to her son.

"Do you have any pain medicine?" I ask the other

attendant.

"Lynda," she says, pointing at herself, "yes, rosewood liniment. We use it for cuts and scrapes."

"Do you have it in liquid form?" I ask.

"No, it's hard to liquefy. It can take days."

"True. Pamela do you think anyone in the marketplace has white willow bark? Or maybe even Arncella. You might know it as Virgin slipper."

"I can have someone check," she motions to another worker who immediately runs out the door.

"Lynda give me some of that rosewood liniment, some ash from the stove and some of the oil you use for cooking."

"What are you doing?" Miriam asks.

"I think that I know what's going on but first we gotta stop these lines. They're the infection. And the mix I'm gonna make will halt them at the bend of the elbow. Next, Kyrie needs to describe to me exactly what he touched. Maybe Cleary can get me some of it. If I'm right, he'll be ok," I say.

"And if you're not," Pamela asks.

"I can make him comfortable."

Cleary arrives barely out of breath and with him the two women we sent earlier. An older man, known around the compound as the Medicine Merchant, follows behind

DC EDWARDS

the trio. I think he's pretty much a quack. But I've seen his cart. He has useful stuff in it, but he has no real idea how to use any of it.

"Your girl wanted to buy some things from me," the man says, a sly smile creeping across his thin lips.

"We need White Willow bark and Virgin Slipper. You have them in your cart. I've seen them."

"Yes, but only a tiny bit and I will be going to another clan in the morning my supply is running low and I promised to be fully stocked."

"Listen bastard," I say, snatching Pamela's knife from her holster and putting it to his throat, "this is no time for childish games. I will gut you and take everything in your cart, you fucking pig. Give us the herbs that we need, and we'll compensate you."

Cleary gently pushes me back. And drags the Medicine Merchant out the door to his cart, which I can see, is parked near the entry.

I quickly mash up the rosewood liniment, ash and oil then I take strips of bed sheet and wrap a tourniquet right below each elbow.

"This is gonna hurt buddy," I say before I cut into his arms. He whimpers, just a bit too weak to scream. I slather the mixture into the cuts then wrap them up with two more bandages. Cleary returns with the Medicine Merchant and the supplies.

"The lines are disappearing," Pamela gasps.

BRIGHT CITY

"Yeah but not for long. This medicine is temporary so that Kyrie can form sentences. I need him to tell Cleary exactly where he was."

"Kyrie, were you in the patch again?"

Kyrie nods sheepishly. Pamela presses a fresh towel to his mouth then gives him a sip of water.

"Kyrie, you have to tell Abigail what you saw and where you were at the patch."

"Last thing I remember was chasing a rabbit. It was fat. Good for dinner. A surprise for mom. I went through a bush. With red flowers and leaves like four-leaf clovers. Not so lucky."

"Fucking Passion wood vines," I mutter.

"Passion wood vines?" Cleary asks.

"Yeah, you might have a different name for them. But when you get a scratch from one of the thorns you get hyper for like a day or two. Elevated speech, playful, happy, euphoric energy and then you crash."

"That sounds like Kyrie all the time, though," Miriam says.

"Yeah, but did you notice anything else?"

"He's a boy. Wants to be like his brothers, always chasing after them. He always has scratches and burns and bumps and bruises."

"Cleary can you turn him over. I think he might have

the thorn in him still. At least a piece. We need to look at
the base of his neck or spine."

I search for the piercing and find a tiny piece of the
thorn lodged just above his tailbone. I take Pamela's knife
and dip it in the liquefied White Willow bark from the
Medicine Merchants cart then gently dig the piece out of
his back.

"Cleary," I say, "you know where this place is? I'll
need you to get me some leaves from the vine. We'll have
to boil them and make a broth. How long will it take you to
get there and back?"

"About an hour."

"Be careful; I don't want to have to treat both of you.
Try not to touch the vines. If you can clip the leaves
without touching the vines, the thorns won't come out."

I turn away from Cleary as he runs out the door. I put a
poultice of the ash mix on the site of the wound then cover
it with clean bandages.

Pamela, Lynda, and I flip Kyrie over on his back.
Miriam gives him another sip of water.

"The vines stung him?"

"Kyrie probably just ran through them which is why
they stung him. It's a defense mechanism."

"Will he get better," Miriam asks.

"I'll make the broth, and we'll feed it to him every
couple of hours for the next day. I can't guarantee anything

because I haven't seen someone this sick from the poison. But I'll do my best."

Pamela pats my back and nudges me away from the bed.

"How do you know all this?"

"I'm a Tracker. That's my job in my Colony. We learn about plants and how they mutated, the cures for different diseases using herbs. It's useful when you're in the Outlands. Most of the time it's a just-in-case type thing. Just in case you get stranded without food or something, you know how to get water and sustenance. How to survive animal and insect bites, things like that," I say with a shrug.

"You are full of surprises. Perhaps you are useful after all," Pamela says, before pulling me towards the door to pay the angry Medicine Merchant.

Around midnight a heavy hand on my shoulder awakens me. I almost jump out of the chair I have propped against the wall next to Kyrie's bed. He drank the broth three times, and his temperature returned to normal. The streaks on his arms are fading. He seemed to be improving before he fell off into a deep sleep. I promised his mother that I'd stay the night and watch him.

"Well, well, *mole* girl. You have certainly surprised me," Saul says, dragging a chair to sit at the foot of the bed.

"I'm here to surprise you," I say.

"Ha! Still the smart ass even in all the time that you've been here. But it's ok because you finally proved yourself to be useful."

"I can't believe your people never knew about this."

"Everything is not easy like your life in your tunnels. The description of the illness the boy had sounds pretty familiar to my men and me. We've had a few people die from it. We tell the young boys to stay away from the patch. There are lots of deadly things there. Flowers being the least of them."

"Or the least obvious."

Saul nods and looks at the Kyrie. The light from the moon spills across his face, and Saul pats the boy's covered foot.

"My daughter kept telling me that you're special. She wants me to keep you here and not sell you during the Cycle. What do you think I should do?"

"Here's what I know, one day, no matter where I am, I will escape. It's up to you whether it's from here or from somewhere else."

"You have nowhere to go."

"I know. But I don't like being a captive. So I'll take my chances out there."

"You are very stubborn."

"So I've been told."

"Maybe I should let you be someone else's problem," Saul sighs.

"Maybe."

BRIGHT CITY

We sit in conciliatory silence until the sun rises. I check on Kyrie and feed him another round of broth. I show Lynda how to make it and promise I'll come back to show her how to quickly meltdown Rosewood liniment. As the sun rises I climb into bed. I think about Saul, hope he's given up on selling me and gained just enough trust in me so I can find my way out. He can never say I didn't tell him. One day soon, I'm going to walk right out those front gates, and he won't be able to stop me.

CHAPTER TEN

FOR THE PAST WEEK, THERE HAS been an influx of visitors for the Cycle. They've set up camp near the entrance. Pamela welcomes each group. I go with her, carrying packages to each leader that she's handcrafted. The week has proceeded with rowdy trade discussions, drinking, and games. Pamela told me this is a significant time for the Outlanders. It's centered on an ancient tradition called Thanksgiving. She said that because the winters are harsh most of the Outlanders wouldn't be able to make it back to Knute for trade until the spring. So they come for the week to celebrate, trade and settle disputes. They return when the ice breaks in the spring. Pamela tells me that tonight she and her servant girls will help me get dressed. Tonight is my initiation into the community. The servant girls giggle as they run brushes and combs through my tangled curly hair, weaving it with ribbons. Pamela pulls out a variety of dresses from her closet, and she talks incessantly about a leader named Victoria who arrived late yesterday. Pamela interlaces the back of the navy colored dress she's chosen for me; I think about the woman that has flustered her so much.

BRIGHT CITY

Yesterday, Pamela pulled me from shucking corn in the longhouse, excitement flashing through her pale eyes.

"She's here," Pamela said, as she pulled me to my feet.

I tried to keep up with her as she practically ran towards the visitor tents.

"What's the rush?" I asked.

"You'll see," she said, giving me a sweet smile.

We stopped outside one of the largest tents in the visitor's campsite. It was different from the other caravans in every way; gaudy and lavender colored with gold accents along the trim. The lamps anchoring the entrance were clearly advanced technology, and I wanted to examine them further.

"We're here to welcome her," Pamela said to two men in long black cassocks and dark glasses standing at the entrance to the tent.

"Come in, sweetheart," a feminine voice echoed from beyond the folds of the tent.

"Welcome, Victoria, thank you so much for coming," Pamela said, passing the basket to the woman.

Victoria tossed her red mane and smiled. She kissed Pamela gently on the lips.

"Thank you for inviting me; I know you had to fight Saul for my place at the table. I think he's still bitter," Victoria said.

"You broke his heart," Pamela replied.

"He's a rascal," Victoria said, waving her hand towards the two chairs around a small round table at the center of the room.

Pamela spent the next 20 minutes regaling Victoria with gossip about the town and the other leaders who arrived earlier in the week. Pamela gushed, and Victoria laughed at all the right parts. I watched their body language. Victoria kept her hand very close to Pamela's fingertips. At times she would touch them, causing Pamela to shift a bit in her chair and stumble over her words. Still, occasionally, I would look up from the knitting that Pamela gave me and see Victoria staring at me. When we prepared to leave, Pamela asked what color Victoria was going to wear that evening. She pulled out a black leather jacket with navy colored sleeves.

"Promise that you and your servant girl will wear something to compliment me tomorrow," Victoria said before we left the tent.

Pamela's hands brush across my shoulders and my eyes focus on my reflection in the mirror. The navy colored dress is long, the hem nearly touching the ground. These clothes feel strange to me. In the colony, we wear uniforms. Dresses are considered patriarchal remnants of the past. I caress the tight bodice, woven with the same navy-colored ribbons that decorate my hair. I take a breath. Pamela twirls me towards her.

"I don't know what I'm supposed to look like," I say.

"Just like this, like a clan leader's daughter. You look perfect," Pamela says.

BRIGHT CITY

Leaders of the various clans fill the longhouse. Around them are some of their guards, women servers and musicians playing loud, bawdy music. The scent of cooked meat, hearty, spicy stews, and baked bread overwhelms the hot room. When we arrive, Cleary escorts us to the main table at the back of the building. Saul is holding court at the expansive table in the middle. When we pass by Victoria, she smiles, raising her glass in our direction before a man to her left distracts her.

"It took you long enough," Cleary says to us as he pulls out our chairs.

"Why are you worried about it?" Pamela asks.

"You know I hate these things," he says. "You're better at all this socializing. We're better at it together."

"I'm sorry, it was my fault," I say, serving Pamela from a plate of stacked meat.

"Figures," Cleary says as he sits on the opposite side of a larger chair between him and Pamela.

Pamela, over the week, confided who each of the clans is and their specialties. Some are fishermen, others are harvesters, and others are hunters. But the clan Pamela called The Travellers are the entertainers for the evening. There is a man who tells raunchy stories about ancient nymphs seducing god-like men. Children do a tumbling routine. A woman sings a song whose voice is so sweet that at the end more than one of the men around the head table wipes their eyes.

"Ah, thank you Ribauld for bringing your people to

entertain us," Saul says, raising a heavy-looking chalice in the clan leader's direction.

"Tonight we give thanks for our clans. We give thanks for our coming together, settling debts and disagreements, playing games and with, of course, trade," Saul says.

The room bursts with cheering and shouts. I notice that Victoria doesn't move, her full crimson lips set in a sly grin. Our eyes meet; she raises an eyebrow then places a finger to her mouth, nodding in Saul's direction.

"Every year on this evening, as you know, I welcome new people into my clan. But tonight is going to be different. I am announcing the binding of my son!"

Gasps fill the room. Pamela and I both stare at Cleary's reddening face. He glances at us then up at his father who pulls him out of his chair and claps him on the back.

"Binding," I whisper to Pamela.

"Can't be," she says.

"What is it?"

"The Binding is marriage. But he wouldn't bind Cleary to Margot; he hates her," Pamela says, nodding in the direction of one of the servant women. She's pale with mousy brown hair swept up in a bun. Her mother is one of the women we sometimes sit with at the communal fire.

"Oh no, he's going to give him to one of the clan leaders' daughters, he's going to be heartbroken. He's in love with Margot." Pamela says, sighing.

BRIGHT CITY

"My son will make a great chief of this clan one day, and he needs a woman who will breed healthy sons for him. I have found that woman for him," Saul announces. "Tonight we welcome her into our community – Abigail Drexler!"

After the announcement, there are more music, dancing, and games but I can barely hear the celebration through the pounding of my heart in my ears. Saul pushes us together at the table and Cleary spends the evening ignoring me, looking guiltily at Margot. I notice when Saul is distracted, he slips out, pulling Margot behind him. As the night ends, Pamela escorts me back to the house, chatting eagerly about the wedding that she says will take place in late spring when the other clans could return. But it was what happened on our way out of the longhouse that keeps spinning in my mind. As we passed the chieftains table, many of them stopped us and gave me tokens of their clans. A wolf pendant, a silver fishing hook, a bag of seeds and as much as I wanted to run and scream, I copied Pamela's polite demeanor, reminding myself that technically I am a clan leader's daughter—Vice Regent of the Drexton Kingdom. I noticed that Victoria was not at the table. As we passed through the door, she stepped out of the shadows, her men behind her.

"So, your handmaiden is going to be your sister," Victoria said.

"It's exciting, promise you'll come back for it," Pamela said.

"Of course, love, I wouldn't miss it," Victoria said, brushing her hand across Pamela's cheek, "but do you think it will happen?"

"Yes, why wouldn't it," Pamela asked.

"I seem to remember hearing that there's another girl who Cleary would rather bound to."

"She could never be the leader of this clan," Pamela said.

"You sound a bit jealous," Victoria said, her lips twisted into a wicked smile.

"No, no, not jealous but Abigail is the daughter of a leader, she carries herself as a leader even as a servant. Margot has only been a servant. The women would never look to her as their leader," Pamela insisted.

"And Abigail is the daughter of which chieftain," Victoria asked.

Pamela stuttered about a clan leader from the east that didn't come who sent me in his stead in exchange for food. I watched Victoria take in Pamela's hastily spat out lie.

"Well, my love, if it happens I will be here," Victoria said before she headed back into the longhouse.

The banging on my bedroom door snatches me out of my sleep. I pull on the scratchy pajamas Pamela made for me and open the door.

"I do not want to marry you," Cleary says, storming into the room. He reeks of alcohol.

"Ditto," I reply, staying near the door.

"She hates me. She thinks that I don't love her," Cleary says, flopping on the floor next to the bed.

"Umm, I'm sure you could work it out," I say.

"No, my father will never let me marry her," he says.

"Why cause she's a servant, or you're a punk ass?" I reply.

" 'scuse me," he slurs.

"You love her. Screw Saul. Why do you listen to him anyway? Don't you guys have some alpha male beat down where the new young male conquers the old one? I've studied those kinds of societies."

"Studied? What are you saying? That's my father. The most respected clan leader amongst all the tribes. If I rebelled against my father, he'd kill me and anyone who opposed him."

"Shit," I say, sitting next to him, "I guess you gotta get married."

"We gotta get married," he says.

"Not if I escape," I say.

"No fucking way," he says stumbling up and moving to stand against the window.

"Think about it, if you help me get away, you can't possibly marry me. Then maybe you'd have more time to get your father to accept Margot. Plus, sounds like your sister isn't too keen on her either."

"What does Pamela have against Margot?"

"She's a servant."

"So are you."

"But I'm not. Not really. I'm a prize. I am a clan leader's daughter. She isn't."

"Pamela doesn't think like that; she's kind and loving to all the women and their children."

"Yeah, they're her subjects but not her equals."

He shakes his head running his palms over his shorn hair. As he paces, I hope I got him to let, his heart speak over his brain.

"Tomorrow night, I'll help you get away. I'll slip you in with The Travellers."

"Will that work?"

"They have no ties to any clan. They're welcome everywhere. Most of their people are runaways from other clans. If you're with them, they'll accept you."

"Thank you, Cleary," I say.

"Thank me on my wedding day," he says.

The explosions rattle my bed seizing me from an already restless sleep. The rat-a-tat-tat gunfire bursts around the small house. I slip out of bed, kick over a table and hide behind it. I hear screaming and shouting then thundering rapid footsteps. I scramble from behind the table and grab my boots. Goosebumps rise across my skin, my stomach curls against the meat and potatoes from the banquet, as I hastily pull on my clothes.

Above the din, boots thump through the house. I search for something I can use as a weapon. But the sparsely furnished room doesn't provide protection.

"Abigail," a voice yells above the banging against the door.

"Cleary?"

He bursts in, knocking the door from its hinges. Victoria, her jade eyes flashing, runs in behind him.

"What's happening?" I ask.

"Never mind. I gotta move you. Dad's orders," Cleary says.

He yanks me up, turns to Victoria standing near the broken door and throws her a hastily packed bag.

"Victoria, here's her stuff. Dad says to move her to the longhouse."

"How about I take her with me?"

Victoria is fast. She shoves a needle into Cleary's neck. He drops at my feet. She slaps a sticky muzzle over my mouth and slips plastic bands on my wrists. I kick her as she pulls me through the doorway. She uses my weight and momentum against me when I try to pull away. She trips me, and I fall flat on my chest. I gag for air against the muzzle.

"Listen to me," she says, pressing her lips to my ear, "I'm taking you somewhere. When we get far enough away, you'll find out why I did this, but you have to trust me."

I glare at her. Then eye the knife she has under my jaw. I want to get away from Knute. I know I'll never have a chance of finding out why my Dad did this to me if I stay here. I need answers. I slowly nod my head.

"Good choice kid," she says, "Now nighty-night."

The pinch of the needle stings against the base of my neck.

CHAPTER ELEVEN

꙳•꙳

WE ESCAPED KNUTE A WEEK AGO. I barely remember being carried through Knute or the trip to this new place. I haven't seen the outside. The windows that let natural light in are thick and frosted. This room is my new prison. It's small like my pod in the Colony. But admittedly more comfortable than anything Knute ever had. I have a small dining table set against the wall of windows facing the city. There is a shelf full of actual paper books, like the contraband I had back home. The twin bed is luxurious. The sheets are always cool and soothing. Even better than my bed back home. Still, even with all this comfort, I feel alone. I feel afraid.

I spent the week thinking about the Colony, my exile, and my father. I mourn Katherine here too. I realize in Knute there was always noise. Welcome noise; noise that kept the memory of Katherine at bay. There was always something to do, always following Pamela. I've dreamt of Katherine every night and felt her arms around me as I've cried. Or I dream of pits full of bodies and Katherine turns to dust in my arms and once or twice I've woken myself up

with my screams. I pace this room and think. I try to piece
the plot together, but it's full of holes I am not willing to
fill. Filling them would be damning my father to hell for
the evil he perpetrates against the Colony and the Kingdom.
But I try to piece it together anyway; forcing my mind to
exist within grays instead of the black and white I've been
taught all my life. Knute showed me grays are the places
where people live. I've seen trades made between warring
clans, kindness where none should be and folk who
survived with the joyous of spirits even while starving. So I
push myself to piece together the story, allowing for the
grays. What I know is someone, most likely my father is
ordering the genetic assassination of colonists. He is exiling
people who find out. He is framing them with treasonous
evidence. But he is having some murdered and selling some
to Clans. Saul confirmed over the three months I was with
his family that he'd bought and sold some of my people,
which means that citizens disappeared right under our
noses. But Saul claimed he didn't know who was making
the trades. He received a letter, on old-school paper, with
names, and skills, nothing more than The Drexton
Kingdom where the signature would be. I suspect marriage
to his son was probably not originally in the cards. He liked
our arguments; he wanted Cleary to have someone to
challenge him. He considered me a prize. Something
maybe he could throw into my father's face one day.
Maybe. But no matter how much I try to piece together this
web of lies. I come back to Katherine, my friend, my best
friend.

And I want to know why. Why to all of it. My sweet,
rebellious best friend is dead. She is dead because she knew
I wouldn't believe her. Still, I pace and ask those questions;
why didn't she confide in me when she first had her
suspicions? When I'm not pacing, I fiddle with a thin black
band around my ankle. It beeps every couple of hours. I

feel my mind slipping. I curl in a corner in the pod most nights, ignoring the bed nibbling at food a young woman named Marina brings. She sits with me in silence, occasionally typing on a small square pad. Tonight she steps into the room with my dinner and opens the heavy drapes covering the single window. She turns on the shower and drops fresh clothes onto the bed. She stands over me until I stand. The shower is hot and soothing. It reminds me of home. I feel the two weeks of sweaty sleep fall off of me. I reluctantly lather my hair and breathe in the minty scent of the soap. In silence, she helps me dress then feeds me a spicy soup she brought for dinner. I sit between her knees, and she brushes the kinks out of my hair; humming a tune. The mournful melody rises and falls. She puts me to bed, a promise of tomorrow in her eyes. For the first time in months, I sleep.

I wake to hear Victoria yelling outside my door. I creep out of my bed. The monitoring device gently scrapes my ankle. I press my ear to the door. I can't make out her words. The large bolt thumps open. I jump back in bed and pretend to sleep.

"C'mon," Victoria demands, "get up. You're not sleeping."

She looks stunning. Head to toe in black, heeled knee-high boots adding three inches to her height. She's slightly over 6 feet tall now. Her auburn hair cascades in a neat but elaborate French braid nearly to her waist. Dark black kohl lines her jade eyes. She looks like a superhero.

"When are you going to tell me what I'm doing here?"

"Maybe today. Now let's go."

I peek around the corner of the open bedroom door. I gasp. The space beyond my small room is floor to ceiling glass and steel. I walk towards the windows. I only had a small view of this brilliant city. Sparkling and animated neon greens, pinks, and yellows dance. I touch my hand and head to the glass. I marvel at our height. I read about skyscrapers for history class. I feel dizzy as I watch the traffic below, streaming against one another. Victoria is sitting at a small square table flipping through several holographic images. My stomach growls as I catch the sweet, spicy scent coming from the food on the table. Apples, grapes, and peaches sit in the center of the full table. There are pink-centered meats I can't name. A chicken dish with a creamy mushroom sauce over biscuits sits on a platter next to other fruits sliced on trays. Marina, who brings my meals, fills my glass. The drink bubbles and shimmers. It tastes like pineapple and ginger.

When I finish eating, Victoria closes the holograms and leans back in her chair. She holds her glass out to Marina who promptly refills it. I nibble on a biscuit, eyeing the redhead.

"Having fun?" I ask.

"Not yet, but soon," she replies before taking a sip.

"Why am I here?"

"Ah, why is anyone here?" she teases. I watch her pick a small piece from a soft, moist cake and put it in her mouth.

"Are you serious?"

"Of course. Philosophical exercises are an excellent

way to keep your mind healthy."

"Why are you playing with me instead of giving me a straight answer?"

"I'm not playing with you. I'm trying to have a conversation with you. That is what good hosts and guests do over food."

"So I'm your guest?"

"Haven't I been more than welcoming? I mean especially compared to Knute's hospitality. You've had plenty of food, comfortable clothing, and a cozy place to sleep. You're clean and presentable."

"If I'm a guest, I can leave."

"Yes."

"Take this thing off my ankle, and I'll go."

She laughs. Her laugh is throaty and icy.

"Oh that, well, that's so you won't get lost. I can't take that off and have my guest lost in this city," she says.

"I want to go home."

"I'm pretty sure you can't do that."

"Excuse me."

"I'm pretty sure you can't go home. At least that's my understanding from your former captors. Let me ask you a question since we're playing a game of cat and mouse. Did you think Saul was going to help you get home? What did you think your life was going to become in Knute?"

"If you don't let me go…"

"You were going to give me an empty threat about your daddy. I can promise you I saved you from a life that would have ended terribly. So be grateful."

"Just tell me why I'm here," I say.

"You are here to serve," she replies as she rises from her chair.

I watch Victoria slip between two glass doors. She gives me a wink as she disappears from view, a sly smile on ruby-red lips.

CHAPTER TWELVE

❧•❧

IT'S BEEN A FEW DAYS SINCE I SPOKE to Victoria. I think about the view from the windows in the open space beyond my room. I find myself pacing in between the busy visitors. They have measured me from head to toe. Yesterday, a woman with an easy smile and a flowing flowery dress spent a couple of hours asking me all kinds of questions. When I asked why she said she measured my mental and emotional intelligence, when I asked how I did, she just smiled.

My mind often wanders back to Knute, how I belonged to Pamela, and until she told me I didn't even know it. How my fate was going to be out of my control. That Saul was going to just marry me off to his son, and I had no say in the matter. I vibrate with anger thinking I'm no better off than I was there. I figured I was free because I could move about the compound in Knute, but I realize that this is just a smaller version of that fictional freedom. I have the illusion of freedom in this small space. Still, I wasn't free in Knute, and I'm not free here. The difference is better food and silkier sheets. But that's no real difference at all.

When Marina appears in my doorway with my dinner, I'm itching for a fight. I've been working to replace remorse with anger. I don't want to feel sad anymore. I want to lash out. I can control this. Although her natural smile has become my beacon to humanity, I want to lash out at anyone. I keep my back to her as she sets my food tray down on the two-seater table. I turn to face her when I hear the slight scrape of the chair.

"Why am I here? What does she mean I'm here to serve? What the hell does she have planned for me?"

Marina smiles. I think about punching her.

"Quit with the smiling! You look insane! Answer my questions!"

She writes on her datapad then turns away from me.

"Are you serious? Aren't you going to answer my questions? You've been sitting with me here. You can see I'm a prisoner. Don't you have any compassion for me?"

I pace the small room trying to ignore tantalizing scents coming from the food on the table.

"Did you know Victoria kidnapped me?" I demand.

I catch her nod out of the corner of my eyes. I can tell she's pretending to ignore me. My face gets hot. I stand across the room watching her. Rage builds in my chest. Who does she think she is? She's a servant! We are both prisoners. Different circumstances, of course, but in the

Colony, we studied how rigid class distinctions destroyed the world. She shouldn't protect Victoria. We should fight together. When she smiles again, I lose it. I cross the room and slap the datapad out of her hands. I stand taller than I have in months. My chest out, I dare her to push back. I shove my diplomatic training, my voice of reason into the darkest corners of my mind. I want to fight.

"Have you lost your goddamned mind?" Marina says.

Her voice is calm, but I step back. She unfolds herself from the chair to stand a full two inches above me.

"Over and over you ask the same question, why? Why you? Poor little Abigail. Are you tortured? A victim? Victoria told me that she saved you from being an arranged bride."

"What does she want with me?"

"Hey, you need to get it together little miss. You're lucky. From what I hear, it seems like you've had a pretty charmed life. Never experienced more than a few hours of hunger, never been in the Outlands without supplies!"

"You don't know my life, what I experienced! My people exiled me for a crime I didn't commit!"

"Yeah, and you landed in the comfiest place possible. I don't feel sorry for you. Victoria doesn't feel sorry for you. No one will feel sorry for you. Now if you want to feel sorry for yourself go ahead. But if you think that will get you out of this room then you better think again!"

"My best friend was murdered!"

"Welcome to the real world, princess! Death is just another thing we have to deal with, doesn't make you special. You survived; you will survive cause you have to. But only if you quit the pity party."

I sit down on my bed. Hot tears coat my cheeks. I hate them. I need to feel tough, but all I feel is terror. I know Marina is right. As a Tracker I studied poverty. But that's all. I never felt compassion. I just felt sorry for those people. Those people. I never thought I'd be one of those people. Then everything was taken from me. Even in Knute, I don't know if I had compassion or empathy. I just felt sorry for them and myself. Now, here I am. I have nothing. I have no one. And yet, I'm not alone, and I've landed in a place most people wouldn't complain about.

"I just...I'm scared. I'm sorry."

I feel Marina's hesitation before she sits next to me. She nudges me with her shoulder then pats my leg.

"I can only give you a few more details. But I promise Victoria will tell you more soon. I'm sorry you're scared."

"I'm sorry I knocked your datapad out of your hand."

"Ha, yeah don't do that again. I've killed people for less."

I glance up. I can tell Marina's serious.

"What if I never get back home?"

"Well, your home doesn't sound that great. But Victoria sees something in you. She's...powerful. And in this city, you're lucky to have a *Danna* like her."

BRIGHT CITY

"Danna?"

"It means patron. She has some business for you. Once you're done paying back your debt, you can purchase your freedom. You'll work out terms. She's fair. I promise it will be an adventure. Now I'm not saying that you can't be sad or angry. But sis, you're gonna have to buck up if you want to have any chance of getting home or better yet, starting a new life in the Bright City."

"The Bright City?"

"Yep," Marina nods, "welcome home."

I wipe the tears off my cheeks and take a deep breath. I know that Marina is right. Why do I want to go back home? I want to know why all of this happened. But will I really get any answers? I look around the room. It's so similar in size to my pod. I think about Katherine. She would hate how I am acting. She'd think my behavior is beneath me. If anyone would want me to push forward, to explore, to live it would be her, Katherine wasn't a quitter. In every class and training we ever had she pushed me to dig deep to succeed. In this case, she'd expect me to examine my surroundings and find a way to escape. I take another deep breath then move towards the table.

"So, is there any way we could reheat this?"

CHAPTER THIRTEEN

❧•❧

"Turn around," Victoria says.

I turn my back to her and face the mirror. It's been six months since I've seen the Colony. I touch the intricate braids lining my scalp. I run my fingers along dark folds of silky pants. I've always been slim and athletic. The clothes make my figure appear curvier. Rich mauve lipstick makes my lips fuller. I smile, but it doesn't reach my eyes. I see shadows of my former self in the reflection. More than the makeup, the expensive clothing and shining oiled hair; the girl in front of me has changed. As the days grow longer between my stay in Knute and my new status under Victoria's roof; I doubt myself. I pieced together the unsolvable puzzle of my exile. Twisted it over in my mind so often sometimes I feel my sanity slipping. Marina's welcome visits push me through those nights that I twist myself into a mental pretzel attempting to solve this riddle. Her friendship brought me back from the brink. Even still, I hide my pain from Victoria and Marina. I cry alone in the shower most nights, stifling whimpers against the wet tile. I accept I am a pawn. I accept I was complicit in Katherine's murder. I accept that my father is a murderer and human trafficker. I accept I'm Victoria's servant—for now.

"You're going to make me rich, my dear," Victoria says.

"Glad I can help."

She laughs and jumps up from her seat. She runs her hands along my shoulders, adjusting the soft V-neck button down shirt.

"Marina, tighter here and here," Victoria says, cinching her hands around my waist then pointing to my bust line.

I blush.

I look beautiful, but there are hints of dark circles under my eyes. I think about last night when Victoria came into my room and leaned against the door. Her arms crossed over her black silk shirt; legs crossed at the ankles. I study her whenever we're together. She moves with fluid determination, different than any person I've ever known. Still, she stands there, and we look at each other for what seems like hours. Then she breathes a sigh, pulls herself up off the door and walks towards me.

"You're leaving us soon," she says.

"You're letting me go?

"In a sense."

"When?"

"Have you thought about what I do; for a living that is? I'm what we call a Broker. I trade information, things...people. It's what we call The Exchange."

"You're going to trade me?"

"Yes, I'm going to sell you to the highest bidder. You are worth quite a bit of currency, information, and power."

"You can't make me do this."

"You don't have a choice. Understand, Abigail, that if you don't go along, you won't have to worry about what will happen next because let me give you just a quick recap. You were lucky in Knute. A clan leader who wanted you to marry his handsome young son protected you. You were very lucky. But I can show you a side of the Outlands that will make your skin crawl. And I know you don't want that."

"You don't scare me."

"Oh I know I don't. But I heard about your little scrap with that fat bald guy. What was his name? Ivan, I think. Yeah, I know a clan full of Ivan's. And I will sell you to them. I will take you to their tribe, and I will sell you to them for a young woman who'd rather live in wealth than in squalor, who's tired of being passed around from one Ivan to another until she's broken."

My breath trembles as I pull myself up to my full height. I am the Vice Regent of the most powerful Kingdom that ever existed. I can't let this break me.

"I guess I can't argue," I say.

BRIGHT CITY

"No, you can't."

"Senator Russell confirmed dinner at nine," a computerized voice announces.

"Excellent," Victoria chuckles. She pours herself a drink from a wine carafe carved out of glass and gold.

Marina touches my shoulder as the dressing platform descends flat to the floor. She points towards a pair of shiny black knee high boots. I slip on the boots and stand in the mirror. Victoria dazzles in sparkling purple, and I am, in jade, the color of her eyes. We match perfectly. In quiet moments alone, Marina tells me I should trust Victoria. We argue. I don't trust Victoria, but I have no choice. I could fight now and lose. Or I can play along; be smart, savvy and find another way to escape. I have to survive. Katherine would insist that I survive. My father would remind me that I am the Vice Regent of the greatest Kingdom that ever existed on earth. I shove his voice out of my head; I will play the game in spite of him. I cling to Katherine's memory, her strength, and her humor.

"Who is Senator Russell?" I ask.

I pull my eyes from the mirror and move towards the picture window overlooking the city. Raindrops creep down the floor-to-ceiling glass, making the reflection of the neon signs wavy and dreamlike. I wonder about the people rushing around the streets.

"Marina, I thought I told you to go over The Apex with her."

"The Apex is the ruling class of Bright City. There are

Ambassadors, who represent sectors in the city and report to the Senators, who make the rules and report to the Chancellor who oversees the whole governmental system. It's very similar to the structure of my Kingdom," I say.

"Very good," Victoria says.

"I mean *who* delicious," I ask, "like personally."

"Ah, well," Victoria, says, handing me a half-full stem less wine glass, "Senator William Xavier Russell, 35 years old, 180 pounds. Brilliant politician—youngest at that level in Bright City. Married to the daughter of his late mentor. No children."

"No children," I say, and then take a sip. The wine is warm and sweet.

"He has connections and money. If he likes you and therefore likes me, then I can write a ticket to any place and space in the city...or anywhere else," Victoria sighs.

"Anywhere else?" I ask.

"There is a whole world outside of the little hole you crawled out of, sweetheart."

Victoria swipes her hand across the viewer on the wall. An image of the former United States pixelates onto the screen. She pulls at the corners of the picture, pulling it off of the viewer and laying a 3D hologram between us.

"This, my dear is your Colony," she says pointing to the northern part of the map.

I move closer touching the red pinpoint she made with

her finger.

"Where are we?"

"Why? Are you plotting an escape?"

"No." My face feels hot as I lie.

"Of course you are. Why wouldn't you? But I know you're not stupid enough to do it under my roof. When you belong to your new patron, you can do whatever you want. In fact, if you have the funds or some juicy information I'll help you escape," she says, cupping my chin in her hand.

"I guess I can't lie to you," I say.

"No, I'm sure you will try to lie to me many more times before I trade you. If you're like me," she says with a wink, "you'll lie as much as possible."

"Maybe I'm not like you," I say.

"Ha, maybe," she says.

She spends the next hour showing me the map. Twisting and turning it, pointing out how far away we are. We're in what used to be Seattle she says. And Knute was near what was Portland, Oregon. I watch her excitedly talk about all the places that exist in this world that I'd grown up believing was absent of real humanity. She talks passionately about what she calls "free cities:" Section Two on the west coast and Idyllic in the southeast, in what used to be Atlanta.

"Now you know what I mean when I say that your plans to run aren't possible."

"This world, there's so much. You knew about the Kingdom."

"Everyone knows about your little Kingdom. It's not a secret. Circular mile-high walls in the middle of nowhere? You think that would go unnoticed? You can't have believed your people were a secret."

"Well...I..."

"You did, didn't you?"

"Our Prophet's predictions secluded us, protected us during The Fall," I stammer.

"Yeah, your 'prophet' might've protected you, but life moved on. You're lucky you got out of there."

"I wouldn't call this lucky."

"Yeah, I guess at this point you wouldn't."

I watch Victoria sashay from the window towards her room shouting orders. I press my head against the window and take another sip of wine. I close my eyes against the tears that threaten to ruin the kohl eyeliner. No more tears. No more feeling sorry for myself. It's clear that I'm going to have to use all my training to my advantage. People are nothing if not predictable. I will figure out Victoria's game. I will find a way out of bondage. And I will escape this place. I'm a trained Tracker. I can live in the Outlands for days with only a thimble of water and a penknife. This game is nothing.

"Suck it up, Abigail, play the game," I whisper.

CHAPTER FOURTEEN

∂•∾

I **'M HAVING FUN. I HATE MYSELF FOR IT.** Senator Russell arrived three hours earlier with two men dressed in identical black cassocks, slacks, and dark glasses. Senator Russell took control of the room the moment he arrived. He complimented me, Victoria and Marina on our outfits, our hair, and the décor of the apartment. He is handsome: olive-skinned, with piercing dark almond-shaped eyes, full lips, and pronounced cheekbones. He favors pictures of ancient North American indigenous people I studied in school. His one flaw, if I can call it that, is a scar that starts at his temple and ends below his chin. Since he arrived, I've wanted to touch it. Victoria warned me earlier that he is sensitive about the scar. She confided he wouldn't appreciate questions about it. It's the first thing I ask when the conversation lulls.

"Quite inquisitive," he says in between sips of wine, "I'm sure Victoria told you not to ask about my…battle scar."

"Who cares what she thinks?" I reply, pouring more wine into his glass.

"Ahhhh, you have a good one this time," he laughs.

I glance at Victoria. For a brief moment, her lush lips set in a firm line.

"This time?" I ask.

"Yes, Victoria is known to introduce young women to the company of those of us in The Apex."

"Only when I find an exceptionally gifted specimen," Victoria interjects.

"Or only when you can steal one," I snip.

"Ha," he says, leaning back in his chair, "Damn, you have got a feisty one on your hands."

"So you've met other young women then?" I ask.

"No, I've never been interested. But I was intrigued when I heard a bit about you."

"My reputation has proceeded me," I reply.

"I get this invitation and find out I'm last on the list to meet you. Why is that?"

"You said it yourself. You've never been interested," Victoria says

BRIGHT CITY

"Tell me, Abigail," Senator Russell turns towards me refilling my glass with wine, "what did you think of Ambassador Snyder?"

Victoria smirks. I pause. Three days before, Victoria invited Ambassador Snyder for lunch. I was shocked when I saw him. He was my age, tall, gangly and very shy. Victoria spent most of the time flirting with him and engaging him in a political debate on the rigid class divisions between The Uppers, The Middles, and Prolets. When he talked about politics, he was animated. He even managed embarrassment when he spilled his champagne. I listened carefully. He is brilliant. But I could see Victoria playing his ego. She allowed him to win one of their arguments; then she praised him for his cunning, even going so far as to say he would rise in the ranks of The Apex quickly, maybe even faster than Senator Russell, who for years had been the youngest ranking official. He tried to hide it, but the thought clearly excited him. It dawned on me. Victoria is playing a game. I'm the pawn.

"Why do you want to know more about a subordinate? Besides I'm sure other people in The Apex are much more fascinating," I say, pouring more wine in his glass.

"Yes, of course, but I'm curious what you think about him."

"I'd hate to ruin this evening with my thoughts about one of your rivals," I say.

"Rival," Senator Russell chuckles, "I hardly think he is."

"Oh, well I suppose Victoria made a mistake inviting him. Who should she have invited?"

"Tricky," he says with a wink.

"No trick. I'm not stupid; I know what's going to happen. So if I'm supposed to be part of The Exchange, then I think I should find out how much I'm worth. I wouldn't want to go to someone who doesn't have a future."

"Abigail, you're interrogating the Senator," Victoria interrupts.

"But you want to get the most out of this Exchange. You said that yourself. How do we find out if we're getting the best?"

"Well, you are going to make someone a great handmaiden. Just enough fire to keep it interesting."

"You haven't seen anything yet," I say.

Victoria launches into some gossip about one of the other Senators we hosted earlier in the week, and Senator Russell attempts to pay attention. But I can feel his eyes following me as I serve more food and fill his glass. I keep my mind on the long game. Escape.

"Abigail, I'd like to know what you think of Ambassador Snyder," the Senator says, putting his palm over his glass as I go to fill his glass.

"I know he thinks the world of you."

"Yes, well, I've mentored him since he was a boy," he says.

"You're like a father to him. I think he was afraid

you'd find out he was here."

"You still haven't answered my question," he says, leaning in slightly.

I look to Victoria, who leans back into the couch and shrugs her shoulders.

"To be honest, Senator Russell," I say, scooting a bit closer as if I am confiding in him, "he's too quiet, too shy and a bit stuffy."

"Ah," he leans in so that our eyes meet, "so you aren't intrigued?"

"No," I say, "quite the opposite. Ambassador Snyder is brilliant, well-spoken, and he has no other commitments. Well, other than to his work."

"Climbing the ranks is a lonely job that only wiser, more experienced men, can appreciate."

"Maybe, but if he works hard, he could have a long and more prestigious career because he is younger than you. He has plenty of opportunities to do so, don't you agree?"

Senator Russell leans back in his chair frown lines deepening his forehead.

"If you'll excuse me," I say. "It was wonderful to meet you, Senator Russell."

Two hours later, Victoria enters my room. She pulls long black pins from her hair, and it slides down her shoulders. I sit with my back against the wall on my bed.

My legs crossed.

"You are amazing," she says.

"Thanks," I say.

"You almost screwed up. But Senator Russell loved you."

"I'm glad you're pleased."

"No, really, you are brilliant, you had him eating out the palm of your hand!"

"I suppose I should be proud of that."

"And I knew you'd take the bait about that scar," she laughs, "Genius!"

"I'm glad you're happy about that."

"Damn right I am. It means I was right about you. It also means you'll survive. Shit, you'll do better than survive."

"Survival is better than death."

"Listen," she sighs, "I know this is not what you thought your life would be. But you should thank whatever gods you worship that you're here and not out there."

"I'm sorry," I say.

"No you're not," Victoria smiles, "but you're good."

She pulls me up into her arms. Her body is smells like

warm powder.

"I like you," she whispers in my ear.

Two days later, Victoria negotiates my price. Senator Russell wants to buy me.

CHAPTER FIFTEEN

ॐ•ॐ

THE SCREAMS FROM THE ROOM NEXT to mine fall silent just after midnight. I wince when they begin again just before sunrise. I can't sleep. I push the tears away from my eyes. No crying. Not now. I lean my head against one of the large windows. The living room is the furthest away from my bedroom, the furthest from the screams. My bedroom. I can't believe I think of this place as home. Katherine fills my thoughts again. What if I didn't pick up that disc? Would Katherine still be alive? I think about the list of names on the disc. The exiled citizens who over the years became lost to the Colony. How did this manage to go on without anyone noticing? We believed the Regent. We all trusted my father when people disappeared.

When Victoria comes into the living room, I realize I'm holding my breath. I sigh with relief. The two men flanking her move with purpose and avoid my gaze. I press my head on the window. The rain streaks the colorful neon reflections. The colors blend and slip into a rainbow. But it's the shadows of Victoria and the men, in black cassocks I learned are called Kaiji, the police force in Bright City, looming large against the window that pulls me back to a week ago; to the day of the trade.

Victoria dressed me in my old clothes. I was bathed, and my wrists were bound with thin see-through bands. She seemed less joyful than I thought she'd be. She said she might miss me. Senator Russell arrived with four Kaiji and Ambassador Snyder in tow. I turned to Victoria. She smiled. My stomach clenched.

"We've come to collect her," Ambassador Snyder said.

"*You* haven't come to collect anyone," Victoria replied.

"You brokered a deal with me," Senator Russell said, "but Ambassador Snyder and I agree that we would be foolish to pay for someone who didn't want to be sold."

"So what are your plans gentlemen?"

"Well, she isn't tagged as a citizen yet, so technically she is a ward of the state," Senator Russell said, a crooked smile creasing his lips.

I saw a flash of the handle of a gun at Ambassador Snyder's waist and stepped back. I remember the feel of Marina's hand on the small of my back. But her eyes remained on the Ambassador and the Senator.

"Are you gentlemen going to try to *take* my property?"

"Consider it the starting point to a mutually beneficial exchange of goods," Senator Russell said.

"And what am I getting in return?"

"Your life," Ambassador Snyder replied.

"Kaiji, bring her here," Senator Russell ordered the men behind him.

"Be assured; Senator, you are not walking out of here with her," Victoria said.

The next few moments happened in a flurry of action. The two Kaiji standing directly behind him grabbed Senator Russell. The other two Kaiji disappeared behind me and brought out a handcuffed woman. Her muffled screams held at bay by a familiar sticky gag.

"Olivia!" Senator Russell yelled. He struggled against the men's grip.

A smile crept across Ambassador Snyder's lips as the realization of the scene played out in front of me. Ambassador Snyder moved next to Victoria. His arms crossed triumphantly. Something cold and calculating and evil replaced the soft and uncomplicated sweetness in his face.

"I've dealt with men like you all my life, Senator. And if there's one thing I know, there's always an upstart looking for an opportunity," Victoria said, patting Ambassador Snyder's back.

"Let my wife go now, or so help me you will all die!"

"Oh, you cut me out of a deal. Now you will deal with me. Until I hear a price that I like I'll keep your wife or maybe I'll let Ambassador Snyder here bid on her first…"

"Shall we start at your office in the Kaiji headquarters?" Ambassador Snyder said a slick smile danced across his lips.

Marina's hand on my shoulder pulls me out of my memory. I notice the quiet. No screams no muffled hurried whispers, just the low hum of electricity. She pulls me to the table and silently pushes a bowl of oatmeal topped with berries in front of me.

"Abigail."

Victoria leans on the doorway. She's a darker version of herself. Dark wet spots cover her black clothes; her bright jade eyes are a dark forest green nearly black. I hesitate to move. The grimace on her face makes me think better of ignoring her.

"I'm tired," she says, slouching in the chair opposite mine. Marina sets a steaming cup of the same succulent nutty liquid I'm drinking in front of her.

"Torturing an innocent woman is tough," I say.

"You'd think hearing screams in the next room would smarten you up. But that's why I like you kid, you're like me, always the smart ass," Victoria says before sipping her drink.

"Where is Ambassador Snyder? Making you do all the dirty work?"

"Ah! The good Ambassador just got an interesting assignment to Knute of all places."

"What?"

"Abigail, you'll find that I am a woman of my word. I always align all the pieces on the board. I protect myself and my interests first."

"You had him sent to Knute?"

"I had to pay my debt, didn't I? I mean I stole you from Saul. He was mighty pissed. Even sent a group of hunters to get you back. But Senator Russell and I thought this would make a good trade."

"I don't understand."

"If you live long enough, maybe you will."

"Is she still alive?" I ask, nodding towards the rooms behind her.

"See for yourself," Victoria says.

She pushes a small gold box in front of me. I stare at the gilded old and delicate carvings. I hesitate. She nudges the box closer.

"I don't think so," I say shaking my head slowly.

"No. You want to know who I am. What I will do to anyone who crosses me. What is in this box is nothing short of what The Apex will do to me, to you, to anyone. Now open it."

I smell iron before I look inside. I remember the scent well. The marketplace in Knute, the butcher, the bloody meat hung on hooks behind him as he swung his cleaver, blood sprayed an already blood splattered apron. My

BRIGHT CITY

stomach turns. I look inside the box. On the purple velvet pillow is a woman's left hand.

I don't make it to the toilet. Marina cleans up my vomit as I back away from the table. I stumble back against the wall of windows. Tears sting my eyes. What kind of madness is this, I think.

"Now you know," Victoria says.

"Why?"

"Understand this; you have no idea the kind of people I'm saving you from."

"She is innocent! I'm innocent! You've trapped us in this game you're playing!"

"Innocent? You don't know shit about that woman," Victoria yells, jabbing her finger in the direction of the darkened hallway. "You don't know what she has done to young girls like you. What she did to Marina before I bought her, healed her."

I look in Marina's direction. She nods slowly. My heart throbs in my chest. I slide down the window and curl into a ball. I force the sounds in the room out of my head until they are distant and muffled.

The elevator bell wakes me. I struggle to sit up; my muscles burn as I uncurl. Marina puts a hand on my arm and shushes me with a finger to her lips. She drapes a blanket around my shoulders and presses a damp towel to my forehead. My mind, now awake, zips through my thoughts. I think about the moment Ivan had me on the ground. I wanted to escape then; I fought to get away. I

143

remember the young girl in Knute that I fought to save from slavery. Should I fight for this woman I don't know? Or should I worry about myself, wait and watch…be silent. I've learned to be an observer. As a Tracker, we observe and report. But I've been breaking those rules. I'm no longer just an observer. I have nothing to lose. What is the worst that could happen? The worst is Victoria sells me, and I become a slave to some clan in the Outlands? Yes, that is the worst. What would Katherine say? She'd tell me to sit my ass here and be smart. She'd tell me to be aware, to observe, then move. She'd look out for my safety. Now she's gone. I need to look out for my safety. I don't have to be inactive, but I have to stop acting on impulse. If I'm going to survive this, I have to watch, listen, and plan. I have to live.

Victoria's jasmine scent wafts into the room before I hear her heels click across the marble floor. I notice she's changed into clean clothes. I try to reconcile the two Victoria's, the one who tortured the Senator's wife and this one, with her breathtaking beauty. Behind Victoria, two Kaiji hold the battered Senator's wife, Olivia, between them. My heart aches. Victoria pauses before pressing the pad on the door to unlock the bleeping elevator doors. I notice a silver gun strapped to her thigh as it catches a glint of light. I force myself not to turn away. I need to witness this. I need to see. I need to observe.

"Victoria Cane, you have the Senator's wife," says an angular ponytailed Kaiji in dark glasses as he steps off the elevator.

"Yes, and you have my money and the other documents."

"Yes, ma'am."

"Put the documents on the table."

A shorter Kaiji drops the bulky package onto the table. Victoria slits open the envelope with a knife. She flips through the stack of paperwork. The short Kaiji passes his wristband over hers, then it beeps. The exchange is a delicate dance. Victoria wears her pride on her chest, a shield. The two Kaiji holding Olivia move her towards the elevator. In the briefest moment, Victoria presses something into the palm of the longhaired leader of the group. He gives a nearly imperceptible nod.

"Thank you *Danna* Victoria; we have taken care of your other issue with Ambassador Snyder. Senator Russell has transferred funds to your account as well as a piece of information you'll find valuable."

"Let's hope it's legitimate. Because next time..."

"*Danna* Victoria," he raises a hand, "I've checked it out personally. You will find it most profitable."

As the doors close I see the senator's wife straighten up between the Kaiji. The one Victoria called Roman lifts Olivia's unmarked left hand to his lips as the elevator whisks them out of sight.

CHAPTER SIXTEEN

❧•❧

"Out of bed," Victoria demands.

"Are you selling me again? Or pretending to torture a woman? What is it now?"

"You still don't see the end game?"

"I'm tired," I say, pulling the blanket over my head.

"Today is a new day. I have plans for you."

Victoria snatches the blanket away and pulls me up to face her. I notice she's casually dressed in jeans and a t-shirt. Her auburn hair slick and in a ponytail, no makeup, all black but nothing showy. She pulls me close enough to see the tiny sprinkle of freckles across the bridge of her nose.

"Your plans haven't exactly been a picnic."

BRIGHT CITY

"First, a shower because, my dear, you smell. Then breakfast and then your new role!"

"Role?"

"Later. But first," Victoria signals to Marina who quickly snips off the bulky ankle monitor.

"I'm free?"

"Oh, well, we implanted a tracking device while you were sleeping, but yeah…you're free," Victoria says as she sweeps out of the room.

"Time to work," Marina says, throwing a pair of boots towards the closet door and a black bag on the end of my bed.

"What…"

"Today, you go to the ground."

We have electricity in the Colony. We use a combination of the wind, nuclear and solar energy. We monitor power usage and curfews, so we don't overheat our various systems. When I step out of the glass and metal doors of the building I realize the Bright City lives up to its name and then some. I gaze at the neon greens, blues, pinks, and yellows that line the long streets. I watch images on signs dance, twirl, burst, then recombine. The wet streets reflect the lights from the signs. I look up and down the bustling street. Buildings tower to the clouds above us. This city reminds me of postcards I found on a tracking mission. Urban, they called the skyline. Marina laughs then pulls me through the throngs of people. I grasp her hand harder and try not to trip over myself.

We pass by street vendors bragging about their wares in front of neon signs touting dancing women. On several different corners, we push through crowds surrounding street performers, acrobats, and drummers, dancers, and singers. Around us, the air is hot and filled with the aroma of food from carts and wafting out of busy restaurants. Above us, trains zoom through glass tubes; Marina says they connect the whole city. As we move further into the city, the signs look refurbished. Some of the bulbs are not as bright. Some are missing. All the signs, written in different languages: Chinese, Japanese, Arabic, English, Spanish, Korean all occupying the same street, blinking wildly. Trash marks the corners of buildings. A film of dirt seems to cover everything. Marina dressed us in matching black jeans, calf high boots, and maroon short-sleeved shirts. As she pulls me along, I notice that the people around us are similarly dressed, but no one has a maroon colored shirt.

Marina pulls me to the side at the mouth of the main street and plops me down on a cold marble bench.

"Stop. Stop. Stop. I have to know about that woman. Senator Russell's wife."

"Hush, what you need is to get some discretion."

"Discretion?" I ask.

"Discretion. Victoria has power," Marina whispers.

"You said, Olivia, was an evil woman. Victoria showed me a fucking hand, but that woman didn't lose her hand. Tortured screams came from that room. But when she got on the elevator her hand wasn't gone, she wasn't bruised or battered. What's going on here? You have to tell me. I feel like I'm going crazy."

"It's true, Senator Russell's wife is an evil bitch. But she had a score to settle with her husband. In exchange, Victoria got some information, funds, and Ambassador Snyder's exile. And Senator Russell's wife got to see her husband pay for some indiscretion between the two of them. We just pulled an almost impossible Exchange."

"I don't understand. But the hand…her screams…"

"You can Exchange for anything in the Bright City. Body parts included. Now, I have to teach you about the city," she says, signaling to a vendor.

She buys two steaming buns off a cart; the seller clicks his wristband against hers. She hands me a bun and begins to jabber about the people passing by us. I taste the sticky bun; the fragrant treat is packed with meat and vegetables in a spicy sauce at the center. I don't ask any more questions until I scarf it down.

"Each shirt indicates your place in the city. The color on the shirt communicates who's your boss. The insignia on the left sleeve designates whether you're an Upper or a Middle," she says.

"Upper or Middle."

"Yeah, we live above the 20th floor we're Uppers," Marina says, touching the black arrow on her sleeve that's pointing up. "Anyone who lives on the 1st floor to the 19th are Middles. They have a sideways arrow."

"What about this bull on the right sleeve?"

"It indicates our job. Our job is brokering we buy and sell information. Most people call us Brokers. But our real titles are *Saybanto*, which means a servant. We're the lower rung in Victoria's Brokerage."

"There's a higher level?"

"Yeah, look there," Marina nods her head.

I turn to see a young woman heeled boots, black leather jacket with a purple armband and long black braids flowing down her back.

"That's Siobhan. She's a *Chusei*. The color of her armband indicates that she works for the Zhou Brokerage. Our armbands are gold which shows we work for Omni Brokerage."

"How do you become a *Chusei*?"

"Slow down, Abby," Marina laughs, "one step at a time."

"So, as Brokers, we trade in information?"

"We trade in everything but specifically information."

"How do we get this information?"

"We overhear, we see, we trade, we barter in any way we can. We use our bodies and our minds to ensure that we have the most valuable information available. We know everything about everyone. And all information comes with a price. When Victoria thinks you're ready you'll have sellers who we call Clients who will give you information in Exchange for your time."

"Clients."

"We'll talk more about that later. For now, you gather information and input it into your wristband. When you upload it to your datapad or DAT for short; you'll want to decode, encode, decipher and encrypt. This process keeps the information safe. We have our personal codes so that no other brokerage can get the information we have. I'll show you all this later."

"We're like spies."

"Spies?"

"Yeah. Spies used to gather information then sell it to the highest bidder."

"I suppose we are then. Let's go; I have a lot more to teach you. The Bright City is a playground for...spies."

The days Marina and I spend together in the boroughs and neighborhoods begin to blur. I learn quickly that all information comes with a price. She leads me around the city collecting bits and pieces of information that we input it into our DAT's. We tell the Client how much it's worth and buy it. We then sell it to the person damage or help the most. Sometimes, though, we overhear information on the street. That information can be the most valuable. Most people sell their information to a few different Brokers to enhance the Exchange. Somehow Victoria manages to use even the most traded information to her advantage. Every night before I go to sleep, I talk to Katherine, in my mind. I keep focusing on the goal of unraveling the terrible mystery of her death. I know it could be months, years before I can flee. But I keep her at the forefront of my mind. I try to work out escape plans; documenting the Bright City streets in my memory. I watch Marina and Victoria carefully. I mimic their moods. I use my knowledge of being a Tracker to listen to the message underneath their words, and for now, I try to meld into my new life.

Today I have to visit Maury; one of Victoria's regular connects. I've been at this work for six months. I'm getting good at it. I try to hold on to my memories of home. I try to keep things organized. I don't want to forget what happened to me. I have to sort out this puzzle. I hurry through the building slipping in and out of the crowds. Maury's office is in the Aztec Quarter. According to Victoria, the Quarter got its name blocked pyramid buildings. I'm not eager to meet with Maury. He strikes me as particularly skeezy. I knock on his door. His nameplate is crooked and chipped.

"Come in," he croaks from behind the door.

The inside of his office looks like something out of a 1950s noir movie, disorganized chaos. Maury has a barely working fan twirling lazily on a crowded shelf, chairs with the stuffing exposed, prop mementos everywhere. The scent of stale cigar smoke and whiskey permeates the air. Maury is no better. He has oily pale skin and watery eyes. He always looks like he just woke up from a weeklong bender. Marina said it's all an act. She said she'd seen him at parties. He cleans up good. I chuckle at the thought.

"My favorite little info bandit," he says before hacking for a minute.

"Victoria has a favor."

"Of course she does, 'cause I'm indebted to her just like you are girly."

"I wouldn't call what I am indebted."

"I'm sure ya wouldn't. What's the job?"

"Victoria received some Intel about Ambassador Snyder returning to the city. She wants his caravan stopped or at least delayed."

"Huh, never known her to put a hit out."

"Nothing like that; she's thinking flat tires, engine on fire, food spoiled."

"Done."

"There's something else that I think might make this a bit more...dangerous. Victoria needs details on Senator Russell's involvement. I'm sure you know why."

Maury unwraps a piece of gum and pops it into his mouth. I've gotten used to his long pauses. I see wheels turning in his mind. I used to think he was a quack, a kook. But I've come to know him as someone who has just as much information as Victoria. Maybe more.

"Price?"

"Name it," I shrug.

"Tell her I need access to The Apex database for one hour. Now that's settled you can get out of here, and I can go home to the family."

"Maury, if I could come up with the credits could you do some snooping for me."

"For credits, of course."

"I only have a few credits on my band, but I'll give you whatever I got for what you have about Victoria."

"You're playing a dangerous game trying to get info on your *Danna*. And you could get me killed just talking about this."

"I thought you said she'd never order a hit."

"*She* never would. But you never know who's listening. Victoria has a long reach, kid."

"So is that a no?"

"No, that's a yes, but you can't afford what I have so if you happen to find the funds you can have what I got, but you'll never have that much."

"Yeah, so what about it. What'll it cost me?"

"Ahhh minimal dig 300 credits, 10% finder's fee. And a free Exchange with Victoria…on you."

"Whew, that's pricey."

"Yeah, I like Victoria, and I don't want to see her brought down by some lil hot shot."

"I got it."

"I got something else for you," he says.

"Oh? What," I ask, pulling out my DAT.

"Put that shit up. I got something for *you*."

"I told you. I don't have many credits on my wristband."

"Nah, hun this one's free. Cause see I like you and I think you're getting yourself into a lot of trouble."

" 'Scuse me?"

"Yeah, here you are sitting in front of me asking about your *Danna*. You don't know me from Adam. I could have hitters on you right now. That ain't smart."

"Do you?"

"No, but Victoria does," he says as Marina slips out from behind a small hidden alcove.

CHAPTER SEVENTEEN

☙•❧

"What the…"

"A'ight dreaddy pay up so I can go get some beauty sleep."

Marina swipes her wristband across his band then pulls me out of his office. We head down the elevator in silence. My stomach flips. I play the conversation with Maury over in my mind. Marina heard everything. If she tells Victoria, she can only say that I just tried to get info on her. Victoria won't like it. But I can tell her that I'm protecting her information. Getting anything floating out there out of the hands of our competitors and into ours. I steel myself for the onslaught that I expect Marina will unleash. We hop a train then get off in a part of the city we've never been. My mind is racing. When we get to a cross street, I pull her aside. I gotta take a chance.

"I have to get away."

"I know you do."

BRIGHT CITY

"Then help me do it."

"You don't dig into Victoria's past. Not even to barter your freedom. You don't do that," Marina says, shaking her head.

"You don't understand. I know I can't go back to the Colony. But she showed me that map. I can get away from her...get away from here. But I'll need supplies. I'll need one of those cycles, the Kaiji use. I could barter for one. I need to make a home somewhere else. Somewhere safe. You had a home before your kidnapping. You know what I mean, don't you? Somewhere safe, maybe you want to go back to your old home?"

"My home," Marina scoffs, "was in some dusty, dank basement in a bombed out building in Minneapolis. My mother sold me. I wasn't kidnapped. She sold me, and Victoria saved me."

"She enslaved you," I reply.

"Despite what you think, she saved your ass too."

Marina pulls me through crowds then pushes us both into a small yellow motorized buggy.

"Where are we going now?"

"You'll see."

After a few minutes on the main street, the buggy turns into a dimly lit alley. People are sitting and leaning against the walls of the buildings. Most don't look at us as we pass. I notice their shirts are gray. At the end of a tangled maze of alleys, we burst into a large bustling bazaar. Marina

157

scans her wristband across the debit Q-Reader and pulls me
from the buggy, which slows down but doesn't stop. The
sights and sounds of this place are different from those on
the streets we frequent. Those streets smell slightly metallic
layered with fresh rain. Amidst the buzzing of the signs,
people walk with purpose and avoid looking one another in
the eyes.

I breathe in the funky curried scents of the bazaar.
Still, it feels...human. The people around us greet Marina
like an old friend. For a moment, I lose her in the crowd.
All around the bazaar children shout and play while buyers
and sellers haggle in a variety of languages. I thank my
father for forcing me to learn as many as I could. This
language they're using is a combination of Arabic and
Japanese. I listen carefully, eager to understand the
sentence structure. I begin to sweat in the sweltering
bazaar. A lot of people wrap their gray shirts in colorful
cloth. Some of the people are covered from head to toe so
that you can only see their eyes peeking out from between
the fabric.

"We're going further in," Marina says, appearing at my
side.

I follow her deeper into the bazaar, hoping we'd have a
chance to stop at the various booths on the way back. We
pause at the mouth of an alley; red paper lights decorate the
entrance. Marina pushes me behind her as we walk deeper
into darkness.

"Sky Girl, you don't belong here," growls a muscular
natty-haired man, his broad back against one of the walls
legs spread out in front of him.

We stop. Marina crosses her arms as the man pulls

himself up in front of her.

"You hear me, Sky Girl? You don't belong here," the man says again.

I hear the scrape of his feet across the loose gravel before I see him lunge at her. She sidesteps him, and he falls head first onto the wet gravel in front of us. He stands up clutching a piece of glass. A collective gasp expels around us as I notice for the first time there are more people in the alley than I could see.

"Are you here snooping, Sky Girl?" he asks, waving the jagged glass in Marina's face. I tense for a fight.

"Sheesh you are the worst bodyguard ever, Dougie," Marina laughs.

I am enveloped in laughter as the large man hugs both of us. I step away from his hug and trip into a tall lanky girl behind me.

"New recruit huh?" Dougie says to Marina who he hands a gold flask.

"Yeah, I think she's ready."

"Hmmm, you want to see Roman then?"

"I wouldn't come to this godforsaken alley for any other reason, pockface."

"Shiri!" the large man yells at the doorway behind him.

A black haired woman in an intricately patterned red and gold robe appears on a wooden balcony just slightly above the alleyway.

"What Dougie? We're running a business! How many times do I say ring the bell?"

"Screw the bell, Mari is here!"

"Mari?" I whisper to Marina.

"Go with it."

"Hey girl, come up!" Shiri shouts.

The crowd moves aside as we climb the steps to the balcony. Shiri slides open the door, and we walk into a bright red room. Ceiling fans slowly circulate warm, humid air. I follow behind Marina and Shiri who chat with one another, ignoring my presence. After we pass through the first room, we walk past smaller rooms. Passing by the doorways, I see couples half naked. My cheeks burn. In the Colony, we receive comprehensive sex education. We are aware of the facts of life at an early age. By law, we abstain from sex until our pairing ceremony so that we can maintain untainted family lines. We understand the risk. We studied the society before The Fall and how their world became overpopulated and uneducated about procreation. Still, it is one thing to know about it and another to see it. I don't realize I've paused to watch at one door until Marina comes back and pulls me along.

"Never seen that before huh?" the woman giggles.

"No," I say, forcing the embarrassment out of my voice.

"Fresh meat," Shiri says to Marina who turns and

winks at me.

At the end of the hallway, the woman pushes open a door. A cold blast of air drifts across my face as she motions for us to enter. The room is all dark wood and cool blues. It reminds me of a painting I once saw of a piece of driftwood against a clear almost pastel blue sea.

"*Moshi Moshi*," Shiri calls out to no one in particular in a singsong voice.

The room is full of young men and women. Couples wearing silky green and blue gowns occupy each corner. Some are lounging around a bubble machine giggling with one another. Others are entwined silhouettes behind silk curtains. At the center of the room is an antique circular poker table. The green felt is worn and the colored chips a bit gnarled, but the cards look brand new.

"Roman, a package," the Shiri says.

She pushes me forward. Marina giggles behind me. I realize the crew around the room looks about my age, maybe only a couple of years older.

"*Oiye*. Hey, Roman," growls a lanky boy, he's dressed in black slacks with purple suspenders.

"One minute," a voice comes up from the table of bent heads.

I crane my head to see who is speaking; Marina pulls me back.

A second later a loud unanimous shout comes up from the table as the card players throw their heads back with laughter and claps on the back. The group flips chips at one another, taunting and teasing in multiple dialects.

The boy at the center of it leans back in his chair, balancing on only two chair legs. His black hair covers one of his eyes and almost hides a scar that seems to run past his hair and just shy of his jaw. I step back from the table. He's dressed differently, but he's the same Kaiji who escorted the Senator's wife in the elevator.

"You're Victoria's girl, huh?"

"No, but you must be her boy."

"Heh," the boy says, twisting a tiny silver toothpick at the corner of his mouth.

The whole table shifts in their chairs to stare at me. The faces range from pale with sharply slanted green eyes to dark ebony with wide almost clear gray eyes. A bead of sweat trickles down my spine.

"You look like Kaiji. You must be her girl."

"I'm not anyone's *girl*, asshole."

The room suddenly falls silent. I am beyond done playing nice. Then the young man laughs.

"Oh yeah, I'm gonna help you."

Roman throws me an envelope as Marina slips into his lap and gives him a long kiss. I blush.

"We'll get you out of the city as long as you help us with our plans," Roman says.

BRIGHT CITY

"We've been waiting for you to get some fight to you," Marina smiles.

CHAPTER EIGHTEEN

EVERY NIGHT MARINA TAKES ME INTO the
Underground. Prolets call this place home. She
confided that she was waiting for me to recognize
that Victoria has me trapped in the Bright City. She hoped
that I would finally show my desire to get away no matter
what the cost. She tells me tonight we'll talk about the plan.
We step through the doors of Club CREAM, moving
through the throng of bodies swaying on the dance floor.
This is a new world. I often think about my education at the
Colony. Music, indiscriminate sex, drugs, is a symptom of
a corrupt society according to the teachings of the
Kingdom. But my heart beats when I follow her into the
night; I feel like I'm living.

We spot Roman lounging on a couch behind a wall of
beads. Marina springs on him showering him with kisses. I
turn away and take a drink from one of the women passing
by with a tray.

"The time has come to tell you the plan," Roman says.

"I didn't know I was auditioning."

BRIGHT CITY

"Everyone is always auditioning. This is all a performance. We all wear masks," Marina says.

"The Lunar Festival is in six months; you're going to escape then," Roman says.

"You have to get Victoria to trust you," Marina says.

"I don't know if that's possible."

"I've watched the two of you. Victoria has a…thing for you."

"Become her *Chusei*, and she'll give all her trust to you," Roman says.

"You pledge your life to her. You're no longer her servant; you're like her right hand. Her voice when she's not in the room. You would be her heir to everything she owns," Marina says.

"She knows I want to escape. Why would she trust that I'd pledge my life to her."

"You'll have to begin to pretend like you want this life," Marina says, "You'll have to do whatever she says without questioning."

"I don't think I can…"

"Listen, I'm going to give Marina some significant information that Victoria will want. Marina will hand it off to you. The two of you will fight. Marina will say that she was going to use this information to buy her freedom from Victoria. But she traded with you for something else and

165

found out the information that you sold her was nearly worthless. Marina will accuse you of being a thief, but Victoria will see you as business savvy. You'll hold the information but offer it to her in exchange for becoming *Chusei*. Your loyalty to her will impress her. She will trust you implicitly after that." Roman says, raising his glass tumbler with a wink.

"Ok, but how am I going to get away during the Lunar Festival?"

"I'll make sure you are at the Lunar Festival Kaiji ceremony," Roman says, "Victoria will allow it. Her reputation and ego will demand it."

"But you have to do your part," I say to Marina, "If I stop being resistant Victoria will be suspicious. I'll keep being me, but I'll slowly shift so that when I pledge to be her…*Chusei*…it'll feel natural. It'll feel like I was becoming her."

"I told you she was good," Marina says, leaning into Roman.

"You were right; she is crafty," Roman says before taking a long drag off of an electronic cigarette.

Roman and Marina blend into the dancing throng. I lean back on the couch and watch the bodies on the dance floor. I've heard about the Lunar Festival in other areas of the city. Every year, the induction of the new Kaiji initiates is the center of the Lunar Festival. It is the only time that all levels of society interact freely and openly. During the annual festival, young people can petition for entrance into the Kaiji, Uppers freely spend time in the Prolet section of the city, trolling for sex or drugs or gambling or all three.

BRIGHT CITY

Uninhibited freedom but also extreme danger happens during the festival. The city becomes an open market. I wonder if Victoria would trust me that much.

A sweating half-naked young man with purple hair and sagging khaki pants flops onto the couch and passes me a nasal tube, interrupting my thoughts. I shake my head.

"More for me," he says, inhaling.

"Do your thing," I say, downing the last of my drink.

"You're different, you're not Prolet," he slurs.

"Nope, I'm not."

"You're not branded," he says, holding up the back of his hand, the raised skin slick and gleaming in the strobe lights. "You're slumming?"

"No," I say, "not slumming, just getting away from work."

"I see you," he says.

"What do you see?"

"You don't belong here."

"I know."

"You know this place…" he says, his words trailing off.

"What about this place," I ask, shaking him gently.

"This place is wrong," he says.

The boy stumbles off to the other end of the couch and curls up in a ball. This place is wrong, just like home is wrong.

I let Victoria keep me busy with training. Despite my best efforts, I find myself enjoying life as a Broker. Even with the hope of escape ever present in my mind, I like gathering information. It reminds me of being a Tracker. I've done small trades amongst the Middles-a secret here, a turn of phrase there. When I come home, Victoria gives me her trademark smirk and nod as I pass her percentage from my wristband to hers. She's proud of my fighting skills, too, insisting I improve them with additional training in Aikido and Wing Chun.

I spend long hours with Marina learning disguises and practicing pickpocketing and eavesdropping techniques. I've worked hard to get closer to Victoria; spending most of my free time in her parlor listening to her negotiate, listening to her stories about past deals, and asking questions. I notice she's grown to trust me. Victoria reveals her childhood in bits and pieces. The other parts Marina offers. Victoria's journey to the Bright City is darker than mine. On the heels of her father's murder, Saul's father kidnapped her during a raid of houses in a farm area near Knute. He traded her to a group of Barters, the Outlanders version of the Bright City's Broker class. Separated from her mother for the first time in her life, she gave the Barters so much trouble that they sold her as they passed through the Bright City on their way southwest. But one subject eludes me; she's never told me how she purchased her Brokerage. Her life in the Bright City before being a *Danna* is still a mystery I'm eager to crack.

BRIGHT CITY

This evening Victoria walks me into her bedroom to talk about the next step in my training. Her bedroom is dark with dim lighting. The walls are black as is much of the furniture. The only pop of color is a vase of lavender flowers on her glass desk. As she pulls out dresses from her closet, I stare out the wall of panoramic windows facing a growing dark expanse of emptiness surrounding the Bright City.

"Not much of a view," I say as I slip into the shimmery white dress she hands me.

"It depends on what you're looking for," she replies, as she turns me around then shakes her head.

"The city is beautiful, but your windows face nothingness," I say, slipping into a tight midnight-blue dress.

"If you say so," she says, shaking her head again.

"No, I mean, the lights, the movement…the city is full of life, but you are looking at death," I say, struggling with a frilled beige shift.

She helps me out of the beige dress and hands me a crimson floor length gown.

"When you look out there you think about death?" she asks, turning me around then unzipping me.

"Nothing grows out there; danger is out there, starvation, pain. All of that is out there. But here…" I say as I slip into a ginger gown cinched at the waist with a V dipping down to my navel.

169

"You almost got sold to the highest bidder in these walls, and you think out there is more dangerous?"

Victoria laughs. She pulls me in front of a three-paneled mirror next to her closet and fusses with the waist.

"You said you weren't going to sell me anyway so…"

"That doesn't mean that this place is safe. If you haven't learned that by now…I don't know how…" Victoria sighs, a pleased grin across her lips.

The training has rejuvenated my body. The tightened muscles in my arms flex as I turn from side to side admiring how the flowing ginger colored gown hits each new curve. I feel confident.

"When I was out there, away from my home, I was scared. I had no one. So to me," I said pointing out the window, "that's death."

"There's just as much death in here as out there," Victoria says, nodding her approval.

"But in here there's life."

"Survival is in here," she says, handing me matching ginger heels.

"Maybe I don't just want to survive," I say, stepping into the heels with ease.

"Ah, so what do you want then?"

"I want to live like you do."

I peek at her in the mirror. I know I've gotten her attention.

"Good. Your next step in being my Broker is going to happen on your Natal Day."

"Natal Day?"

"Your birthday is in a week, correct?"

"Yes, it is."

"You'll be 18."

I turn from the mirror and face her as she moves towards her desk. She swipes across its surface, and an image of an older man emerges.

"This is Senator Riley. He is going to bid for you on your Natal Day. He has some information that we need. It's your job to get the information in any way possible."

"I don't know what you mean."

"Don't be naïve. Do you want to be like me, Abigail? You want to survive *and* live?"

"I've never…"

"I said any way possible. Figure it out."

CHAPTER NINETEEN

❧•❧

MY NATAL DAY ARRIVES DURING A thunderstorm. I can't see the streets through a thick fog that hovers just below our windows. Marina comes in with my breakfast. She hadn't done that since Victoria cut the tracking device off my ankle. For the first time, I question her plan to get Victoria to trust me. Marina insists, though.

"I can't do this," I say.

"You have to."

"You don't understand I've never...done...what I think she wants me to do."

"I know you haven't."

"I mean she didn't explicitly say I had to..."

"But she meant that you should. The bidding tonight isn't just for your conversation. You know that right?"

I nodded. In the Colony, we're expected to remain celibate until we find our match during The Summoning. My Summoning Day would've been today.

"How could she expect me to do this?"

"It's our job," Marina says.

"But you're with Roman. Do you still…"

"Yes, I have to. Now you have to."

"I'm not going to," I say shaking my head.

"Then don't worry about getting out of here. Because Victoria will never trust you enough to give you the kind of freedom you'll need to escape." Marina says.

I sink deeper into a bubble bath as the young women who usually prepare Victoria washes my hair and scrub my nails. Victoria has made all kinds of preparations for this evening. She's invited many of her contacts. The apartment has been buzzing with activity. At Victoria's insistence, I've spent most of the day cordoned off; away from the activity I can hear beyond the door. I don't want to do this tonight. It's not just that I'm afraid

"Girls, I need a minute alone with Abigail," Victoria says.

She pours warm water over my hair then begins to pull a brush through it.

"Do I have to have a conversation with you about tonight?"

"What do you mean?"

"Do I have to give you the story about the birds and the bees?"

"Birds and bees?"

"Sex," Victoria laughs, "do I have to tell you about sex?"

"No, no, no," I stammer.

"Alright, so you've done it before?"

"No, of course not."

"What do you mean of course not?"

"Well, if I were back home, my 18th Natal Day would be when we'd have the Summoning. It's a matchmaking ceremony. My match and I would marry in a year."

"And do you get to have sex in between the matchmaking and the marriage?"

"We don't forbid it, but very few colonists do it. We have responsibilities to the Colony and our Kingdom before the wedding."

"I see," Victoria says with a smile.

"I mean it's not like some old world, 'it's a sin' shaming crap. It's just we believe sex can complicate relationships and human relationships are already complicated enough. I mean, of course, we experiment and kiss and whatnot, but that's just fun. Real sex is for your life partner."

"Interesting."

Victoria brings over a large towel for me. She wraps it around me then sits me in front of her vanity and runs the brush through my hair. The warm, dim light makes my skin look like its glowing.

"You're telling me that I have to have sex tonight with someone I won't be partnered with," I say.

"Yep, that's what I'm telling you."

"Do you do this? Does Marina?"

"Yes, we do. Although I haven't in a long time."

Our eyes meet in the mirror as Victoria twists my hair into a bun, then pulls a curling tendril down on each side.

"It will hurt because you haven't done it before. You don't have anything to worry about with Senator Riley though. He doesn't expect much. He doesn't give much, but he doesn't expect much."

"Ok."

"The first time I did this, I was with a man like Senator Riley. I was scared. But I knew when it was over I could take a bath, put on clean clothes and walk away. Remember your goal is to get Senator Riley to give you information. I trust you with this."

"I'll do my best."

"I know you will," she says.

She kisses the top of my head and calls for the girls to come back in to do my makeup. Out of the corner of my eyes, I see her watching me. Maybe Marina is right; maybe I can get Victoria to trust me.

Marina and I stand next to the hors d'oeurves and gossip. She points out different members of The Apex, Kaiji, and *Chusei*.

"That group over there, the ones dressed in silk kimonos. Those are the *Chusei*. Well, some of them."

"They're beautiful," I say.

"Makeup helps. Even the boys, wear a little eyeliner, but yes, they're supposed to be the best of the best. They are skilled in every way a Broker needs to be. They can dissect every sentence. They can read lips from across the room. They will use every angle to get information for their *Danna*, and they have no problem getting their hands dirty."

"And our plan is supposed to make me one of them," I say, shaking my head.

"You will be one of them, you have a lot more training, but we'll make you the best *Chusei* that has ever existed in the Bright City," Marina says, clinking her glass against mine.

"We've seen the one in the middle before right?" I ask.

BRIGHT CITY

"The one holding court? Good eye! That's Tinka of the Zhou Brokerage. She's been a *Chusei* for years. She's their unofficial leader. *The Chusei* don't have a clan, but they do have a hierarchy, and she's at the top. When you become a *Chusei*, she's going to be so jealous of you. She wanted Victoria to be her *Danna*. But Victoria wasn't too interested. She likes unique finds, like us."

"Come on, we better circulate, we have information to gather," Marina says.

We split up and move through the party. I make it a point to serve The Apex guests first, spending a bit of time with each of them. I make sure the Kaiji are well fed, and then I approach the *Chusei*.

"Is there anything I can get our guests from clan *Chusei*?"

"We are no clan," Tinka says, rolling her eyes before looking me up and down.

"No, of course not, excuse my choice of words," I say, bowing slightly.

"You're the one we're here for tonight," says one of the male *Chusei* in a red and gold Kimono.

"You're here for Victoria. I'm merely her servant."

"No, he means, this is your Natal Day," Tinka says.

"Victoria has graciously allowed the celebration of my Natal Day," I say.

"Oh this bitch is cunning," laughs one of the female

Chusei in blue and gold.

"Too cunning," Tinka says. "Don't find yourself on the other end of that."

"Thank you all for coming," Victoria announces from across the room.

"Excuse me, have a good evening," I say, turning towards the raised dais.

My stomach clenches as I listen to Victoria dazzle and delight the crowd with her turns of phrase and her sparkling wit. I feel nauseous. I reach for the wine off a passing tray and take a large gulp from the stemless glass.

"Now I ask that we begin," Victoria announces.

The silent bidding builds the buzzing energy of the room. Although everyone is eager to see who bid the most, I'm the only one who can see the offers on my DAT. I kick myself for being pleased with the amount of money and favors the men and women put forward. Marina rings the bell signaling the closing of the bids. I pass through the crowd towards the Exchange room to change as the music and conversation swell. In an hour, Victoria will bring Senator Riley to the Exchange room.

"Abigail, I'd like you to meet Senator Riley," Victoria says, as she escorts a short ebony-hued man. He has a baby face. But I know from his file that he's in his mid-forties. He has a brilliant smile and violet-colored eyes that in dim lighting look nearly black.

"Good evening, Senator Riley. Thank you for coming to my Natal Day gathering."

BRIGHT CITY

"Thank you for choosing me. I know I wasn't the highest bidder."

"You were the youngest," I say.

Victoria smiles, gives me a wink, then closes the door behind the Senator. I step out of my shoes, so I'm not towering over him. When he moves closer to kiss me, I replay this mantra in my head: *This place is wrong. But do what you must do to survive...to live.*

And so I do.

"I've never done this before," I confess. No need to keep this a secret. I just don't know where to start.

"So I've heard," he says, removing his jacket and stepping out of his shoes. I'm suddenly taller than him again. He motions towards the bed, I sit.

"I guess I'm nervous," I say.

"No need, but you are very...strapped in...let's get you out of this..." he motions up and down at my dress.

I stand and begin unwrapping while he goes to the small glass bar and pours a drink. He sits down in a chair in front of me and watches me undress as he sips his brandy.

"Am I doing this right?" I ask.

"You're fine. Beautiful, in fact. I'm very lucky."

I let the dress fall to the floor. I try to keep the embarrassment off my face as I stand there in the black silk underwear Victoria matched with the dress. I think about the films we watched about sex in the Colony, the technical explanation of procreation. There was nothing in the movie about passion. And nothing about the uncomfortable level of embarrassment I'm experiencing in this moment.

"Lay on the bed," he orders.

I pull the covers back and slip between the soft sheets. As Senator Riley undresses, he's a bit paunchy around the middle the shadows of toned abs still keep his belly from being jiggly. His body has scars here and there with a smattering of curly hair at the center of his chest. He looks comfortable. He climbs into the bed on the other side and pulls me towards him. His lips are soft, but his kisses are rough. I follow his tongue with my own. His breath is sweet with brandy; I wish I'd drunk a bit more. He nips at my neck and trails his lips and teeth along the outside of my chemise then pulls it up and over my head so that he can taste my nipples. I moan.

I'd always been a bit of a prude Katherine would say. I had boyfriends. All teenagers in the Colony dated. But very few did anything more than make out. Katherine, the rebel, had sex with Gregory right after she got out of Re-Education. He was a boy we grew up with who was a couple of years older than us. It was right before his Summoning that sent him to one of the Southern Colonies. Senator Riley's hands pull apart my thighs, and I gasp as his tongue darts into me. He nibbles my inner thighs as he pulls the panties off and away.

"You don't have to worry about pregnancy," he says as he places my legs around his waist, "I got snipped."

I nod. I have no words. I prepare for his next step. I hear Victoria's voice in my head; *It will hurt because you haven't done it before.* I close my eyes and take a deep breath as he pushes himself inside me. It hurt. Yes. It hurt.

"Open your eyes," he says, as he pushes himself in and out of me.

I do. And see his smile. He has beautiful teeth, soulful violet eyes. He pulls me to his chest as he rocks in and out of me.

"Move with me," he whispers in my ear.

I slowly catch his rhythm and feel him sliding in and out until I am thrusting back matching his pace. He groans in my ear and lets me go so that my back is against the bed. I keep my arms around his neck even as he seems to go somewhere else. Away from here and in my mind, I move to another place. Strangely, following a memory of Victoria in her bathtub. The water was dripping from her skin, watching her bathe, steam rising from the bubbly tub. Her red hair piled on top of her head while stray wet tendrils caress her shoulders. I moan again, and he begins to thrust harder and faster. He presses his body closer to mine, and his kisses become more urgent more insistent. I reply, surprising myself. He's not here with me in my head. She is. The image of her stepping out of her bathtub. Her hips are slender and shapely. Her stomach flat and glistening with water. The curve of her lips as they turn into a sly smile. I open my legs wider, and he groans louder. I follow the curve of his back, tracing the muscles with my fingers until I reach the top of his butt. His thrusts are slow as he pulls himself out of me.

"I want you on top," he says.

He maneuvers me on top of him. I feel him slip inside

me.

"What do I do," I ask.

"Move your hips," he replies, guiding my hips with his hands.

I gasp. I feel my stomach tightening as I rock with him enjoying the feel of his hands guiding me. I let my mind wander again back to Victoria, her wet nakedness in front of me. And wonder what it is like to taste the water in the hollow of her neck. I feel Senator Riley adjust me again so that I am sitting on his lap. He wraps my legs around his waist, and he buries his head in my chest licking and nibbling my nipples until I feel goose bumps rise across my body. He moves me again like I am his doll, his plaything. My head is at the bottom of the bed, and he's on top of me; this time not slowing down his thrusts is stronger and harder.

"Oh," I cry out.

His moans are like growls as he embraces me tighter. I move with him matching thrust for thrust until he collapses with a loud groan on top of me. We both pant with exhaustion. The ache between my thighs pulsates. After a few minutes, he rolls off of me and pulls me with him towards the pillows at the top of the bed.

"You'll be sore for a little while," he says, putting his arm under my head.

"Victoria said it would hurt."

"Everyone has a first time," he says, before taking a drink and then offering me the glass.

I sit up and pull the sheets around my nakedness. I take the glass and sip the brandy. The sweetness coats my tongue and feels warm in my stomach.

"We have a lot to talk about I suppose," he says, putting his hands behind his head.

"Like what?"

"I have done this hundreds of times. We have an Exchange of information. I brought you a package. It's in my coat pocket. A bit of information for Victoria."

"Oh."

"Ahhh, sometimes when you do your work you will be with someone who will slip and tell you things. But sometimes, it will be a simple transaction. Now, why don't we relax before we have another go, hmm?"

He talks animatedly about his newest project. I nod and smile at all the appropriate points. The second time we do it; it hurts less. When he falls off to sleep, I slip into the black marbled bathroom and draw a bath. I inch into the hot scented water and lean my head back against the cool of the marble headrest.

My Natal Day in the Colony would have been a celebration. We would have had the Summoning, and I would be sitting with my future husband. Most likely, someone, I've known all my life. Someone who I'd have two years to get to know before we married. I would be taking my place on the Council. Everything about my life would have been different. The throbbing between my legs has lessened. I gently touch myself and find that I'm slick still. My fingers graze across the tingling between my legs, and I giggle. My life is different. I'm different. My thoughts wander back to Victoria. I can't fight that I'm attracted to her; deeply attracted to her. Why? I sigh and push myself under the water. I resurface and exhale. I'm not the girl I was when before my exile. I'm not the same person as a servant in Knute. I'm not even the girl I was when Victoria brought me to the Bright City months ago. This girl; this woman, is new. The only way I've managed to survive up to this point is on the skills that I learned when I was a Tracker. I've been surviving with my new skills as a Broker. The only way I'll escape is if I embrace this, all of this.

"Abigail?"

Senator Riley calls out for me from the bedroom.

"In here," I say.

I hear him before I see him. He smiles as he holds open a towel for me.

"You smell amazing," he says, pressing his nose into my neck.

"Thank you."

"Let's go back in," he nods towards the bed, "I got an hour before I have to leave and there are a couple of other things I think you need to learn before you go out into the big bad world."

"Lead the way," I say.

Time to embrace my new life. For now.

CHAPTER TWENTY

&ᴏ•ᴏ&

I PROWL THE BRIGHT CITY ALONE. Each corner opens a new world, and I embrace it. I treat each Exchange like a Tracking mission; digging for clues, harvesting information. I feel alive, more than I ever felt in the Colony. Sometimes, during the midday, I stand in the middle of the throngs of people and close my eyes. I hear their voices, their breathing. They brush past me; each body feels different. The scents wafting around and from the people, sharp and provocative sometimes funky, fill my nostrils and I calm my mind. I peek into the one thought I've had since my Natal Day celebration. How am I going to betray Victoria?

It felt so uncomplicated before I began to have feelings for her. Since my Natal Day I've had an Exchange with a plain looking but wealthy socialite whose body was curvaceous and who taught me about the more intimate sexual relationships that women can have with one another. But I couldn't stop thinking about Victoria.

She doesn't make it easier. She's been taking me to parties as her escort. Dressing me like her doll; spending time lying with me in bed, laughing and chatting about her newest adventure or scheme.

"She's seducing you," Marina said one evening as we made our way to Roman's club.

"You think?"

"Sometimes, you can be very dim, Abby."

"I don't know what to do."

"Whatever she wants, do it. It makes our plan much easier. She'll never see it coming."

I nodded, but I keep the fact that I am falling for Victoria to myself. When Marina told Roman the possibility of a romance between Victoria and me, he clapped and laughed; commenting that the "ice queen" would soon get her just do. They both encouraged me to keep moving forward. I promised I would.

In moments when I have doubts about everything we are planning, I think about Katherine. Her memory keeps me grounded. Knowing it is my job to find out the truth of her murder and our exile fuels me. I learn the streets quickly. I make trades for information swiftly, sometimes recklessly. And every time I return home Victoria welcomes me with a hug and kiss on the lips; bragging about how she made the right choice in keeping me. Each kiss feels like fire on my lips.

Tonight, after a long negotiation with a Kaiji leader for information about two Brokerages who attempted to steal

BRIGHT CITY

one of Victoria's top clients, I sit in the living room watching her personal seamstress adjust Victoria's black gown for what she calls her Mobility Party. The party takes place during the Lunar Festival. Every year, she explains, she brings together selected Prolets and an influential group of Uppers and Middles to mingle and observe them and possibly sponsor them for mobility. Mobility, the movement between the groups, only happens during this one time of the year.

"This is how the Bright City remains stable," she says.

"It sounds incredibly unstable," I say.

"Well, have you ever looked at a Prolets hand? That circular brand with a line in the middle marks immobility. You'd think this inflexibility might cause a revolution. But every year, ten Prolets are selected randomly through the Bootstrap Lottery."

"The Bootstrap Lottery?"

"Yes, Prolets invest in the lottery all year. A few credits here, a bit of information there in exchange for more tickets."

"So what happens? How are they moved up?"

"The winners of the lottery are revealed every year during the Lunar Festival. Out of the ten winners, two are chosen to rise to either a Middle or Upper position. Really, the luck of it all depends on who wants to sponsor them. So usually you'll have a Middle or Upper employer sponsor their Prolet servant. Occasionally, a Brokerage will sponsor a particularly talented or unique Prolet."

"What happens to the other eight?"

"Oh, they are given perks for the year in the form of credits so they can invest in the Lottery again."

"I still don't see why they don't revolt."

"Well, it gives them hope that one day one of their children will move up in a higher caste."

"Who are the Prolets that have managed to maintain their newfound status? And what about the brand? I mean people know they're Prolets and quite frankly I haven't seen anyone treat them with much respect."

"Ah, the brand. Well, plastic surgery can take care of that. But Prolets who move up in this system must maintain a brand for two years. I mean who wants to rebrand someone. As far as maintaining, well there are a couple of *Saybantos* like you and Marina who have managed to hang on at one of the lower Brokerage houses."

"Why won't someone help them?"

"You know what we do. How we make our living. We maintain our status through the power of information. A Prolet wouldn't have access to that power nor would most Uppers or Middles risk their places in the Bracket."

"The Bracket?"

"I thought I told Marina to train you on everything. Bracketing," Victoria says, swiping her hand across the viewer revealing a chart with hundreds of names, "determines your ranking amongst the Middles and Uppers in the Bright City. If you aren't in this Bracket, you don't belong. Every month this chart is adjusted. Our Brokerage moves up or down depending on the value of the information we supply each month. To those in The Apex, it's about the amount of political power they wield."

I move towards the viewer to get a closer look. Amongst Brokerage houses, we're ranked number one with Zhou Brokerage just two points below us at number two.

"So if someone wanted to devalue your information they could."

"Yes, we do that every month through our trades."

"So this is all rigged."

"Yes, but it makes the Prolets happy to live in luxury for a short time. And who knows one day our Chancellor may be a Prolet. If they ever learn to play the game correctly."

"Well, what about you becoming Chancellor one day," I say.

The action in the living room comes to a halt as everyone looks at me. Victoria laughs then pulls me into her arms.

"You are so beautifully naive, but that's why I'm keeping you close to me."

She presses her full lips to mine then wipes her lipstick from my lips with her thumb. Her throaty laugh fills the room as the action picks up. I'm paralyzed. My mind drifts back to my memory of her getting out of her tub; her body dripping wet and I feel the heat rise to my cheeks. There is no reason for me to feel like this. She is essentially my captor, but her arm around my waist shoots heat down my thighs. I want to melt into her. I take a deep breath then step away from her touch and move towards the picturesque windows. The neon seems particularly bright. I try to phase out her voice as she gives directions to the staff.

These new feelings make my plans feel unwieldy and impossible. I doubt myself. What if I can't go through with the scheme Roman and Marina have devised because of my emotions? My love for Katherine pushed me to make mistakes with my plan to help her. And because of that, I lost my best friend. I have to step back from these emotions and figure out another plan. The other problem is I depend too much on Marina and Roman. The more I learn about the city, the more I explore the city on my own, the more I realize that I need another plan. I have to escape here, and I know that Marina wants to escape Victoria too, but maybe I'm too trusting. If I've learned nothing, it's that I can only truly depend on myself. So I need a new plan; one that keeps Victoria from getting hurt and helps me escape. Thinking about leaving now feels painful. But I can't stay here. I can't. For the first time, even as I whisper this to myself it feels like I'm trying to convince myself to leave.

CHAPTER TWENTY-ONE

&•&

TODAY, **WHEN ROMAN SHOWED UP** at the door, dressed in his Kaiji black, his hair in their signature ponytail, I'm caught off guard. The Lunar Festival is in three months.

"*Danna* Victoria," Roman says when the door slides open.

"How are you my dear," Victoria replies holding her hand out as Roman bends at the waist and kisses the top of her knuckles.

"Fine, fine. Of course, there is lots of energy at Kaiji headquarters."

"Of course, new initiates and the Lunar Festival. Exciting times, yes?"
"Yes, yes. That is why I have come to seek your services."

"Oh? Well, I heard that all of your officers have escorts to the induction."

"Yes, well, this request is for a special official. He, well, can I trust you?"

Victoria nods; whenever someone asks can they trust her, she always nods. She never gives a verbal response, always a nod. A nod is deniable.

"A Kaiji comrade of mine will be promoted that night. I want him to have a special escort."

"Ah, Roman, what good news. Is this someone I know?"

"No, ah, I cannot say who. I'm not even supposed to know."

"I see. Then how do you, or I, know it's true?"

Victoria gestures for Roman to sit down on the smaller couch near the door. She sits across from him crossing her long legs. I step further away from the two of them positioning myself so that I can see them both.

"I have proof."

"Verifiable and purchasable?

"Verifiable and tradable. My comrade's promotion is over some key Kaiji that are Senator Russell's favorites. I'm sure you know why." Roman says.

"I never involve myself with Kaiji politics," Victoria says.

BRIGHT CITY

"Of course, *Danna* Victoria," Roman says.

There is a brief moment of silence. It's like watching two alpha tigers in a cage circling one another, looking for weaknesses among the muscles. Searching for a place to strike and wound or maybe kill.

"Marina, can you bring our guest a drink?"

"Oh, *Danna* Victoria, it slipped my mind. My young apprentice is waiting in the lobby. Can you send one of your girls to bring him up? If that is no trouble."

"An apprentice? So soon before the Lunar Festival?"

"He was a…gift…you might say."

"So you have been trolling the trading scene for someone to exchange information with."

"You are my first stop," Roman says as he accepts tea from Marina without so much as an acknowledgment. I'm fascinated by the dance the three of them are doing. I realize the lump in my throat is for Victoria. She doesn't see the setup. She doesn't know the extent of this game, and she doesn't realize that in three months she won't be the number one Broker in the market. If everything goes the way it's supposed to, she will lose all of her connections. Soon, I will be safe and free.

"Marina, be a dear and get the Kaiji apprentice in our lobby. People probably think we're planning a coup."

"Tell me all about the festival. What have you heard of the decorations? The invites?"

"Well, of course, you've received your invite months ago."

"Of course."

I pour tea in her cup then top off his. I move into Marina's place beside Victoria's couch. Roman looks regal in his all-black Kaiji cassock and slacks. Even the scars across his forehead and crisscrossing his jaw make him look rugged and tough. Less sinister than when I first met him. His long hair pulled into the Kaiji ponytail, and his movements are graceful, not aggressive. He flirts with Victoria as he chats about the arrangements for the festival. I find myself falling into my role, listening and taking in the details but also noting the things he's not saying. The things Victoria will want to talk about when he leaves. He doesn't mention Ambassador Snyder although we know he will be at the Lunar Festival. Roman doesn't discuss Senator Russell's issues with Victoria. Victoria never asks why he would come to her knowing her presence will be problematic for Senator Russell. More importantly, he doesn't mention the Chancellor who we'd heard was going to make a rare public appearance at the Festival. Victoria's contacts in The Apex didn't have this information. We'd been scouring all the communication lines across the city for why the Chancellor is going to make an appearance. No one seems to know why or when. None of us look up when the door beeps then slides open.

"So as you can see the festival will be bigger and more elaborate than ever," Roman says, taking a sip of his tea and waving me away from his cup before I can refill it without otherwise acknowledging my presence.

"*Danna* Victoria," Marina says, using Victoria's

BRIGHT CITY

formal title, "I'd like to introduce Kaiji Roman's apprentice."

Victoria stands and smiles. Roman steps up next to the hooded apprentice. Roman pulls the hood back, and against my better judgment, I audibly gasp.

"*Tyro* Cleary," Roman says.

CHAPTER TWENTY-TWO

❧•❦

CLEARY BEING IN THE PICTURE WAS NOT in my plans. But he could make a good distraction for Marina and Roman. I realize their plan is more about revenge against Victoria than about me escaping. I try to find out why Roman is so intent on ruining Victoria, but he stonewalls me with jokes and claims that it's because of Marina. But I know vengeance when I see it. He's hiding something, and I don't think it's just from me. I feel like Marina has no idea what's behind his motivations. Formulating an alternative plan to escape hasn't been easy, especially now that Cleary is back in the picture. A week after Roman revealed him to Victoria; he was at Roman's weekly card game. We waited until they finished and Roman dismissed his friends to talk about the next steps in the plan.

"What the hell, Roman?" I said, pointing at Cleary.

"Ahhh c'mon Abigail didn't you see Victoria's face? She was stunned. It got to her to see Cleary here."

BRIGHT CITY

"This is bullshit Roman! How did this happen?"

"Roman has his reasons," Marina said, embracing Roman.

"No, no, no! We are a team this does not work if we're keeping secrets from each other," I said.

"Keeping secrets, you're good at that," Cleary muttered.

"I don't know what the hell you're talking about, but you're not supposed to be here," I replied.

"You and Victoria made my father look weak to the other clans! We've had to fight to hold on to Knute. I'm here to make things right!"

"So what are you gonna do? You can't do shit!"

"I have a plan."

"Oh, now he has a plan, how does that work with our deal Roman?" I demanded.

"Simple. *Tyro* Cleary here is going to help you get out of the city."

"Here's the problem, didn't we already have a plan to get me out of the city? I feel like you three left me out of the loop."

"He's technically going to get you through the Outlands," Marina said.

"Cleary is your escort home. Marina and I have other

business."

I knew then that I'd been right to devise my plan. I walked away from that meeting more determined to get away and to find a way to do it without betraying Victoria. Whatever Marina and Roman had in mind for her I didn't want to be around to see it. The new version of the plan had Marina getting me to the ventilation tunnels and Cleary escorting me through the Outlands. For his part, he'd get a king's ransom of materials to trade and credits to exchange for more materials within the Bright City, enough to pay off the clans and make up for the damage to his father's reputation. But even that is too simple. Still, I let them talk me into it. I knew I wouldn't go along with that plan.

Tonight I finalize my new plan. I toss and turn with the reality that I'd let Roman and Marina's plan go too far without me paying attention to all that was happening. I'd been a pawn in this game for too long. I mentally scroll through my plan again, adjusting for Cleary as the new variable. The Kaiji Induction ceremony is too perfect. There're too many opportunities to be spotted, and I can't let Victoria know I'm leaving. But more importantly, I can't be near Marina and Roman so I opt to escape just after the ceremony when I'd be with my escort. I'd managed to get a tinsure of Noxine, a quick-acting sleeping drug. I'll give it to my companion in the cab on our way from the ceremony. I'd have him stop at Nippon Emporium, a fetish shop, to pick up a package and I'll slip through the back while he's knocked out in the cab. After paying Persus, the manager of the shop, a hefty fee, I was able to see the plans of the building. It has a back door that leads right to an alternative ventilation system that pointed towards the ocean. I'd have to take the long way around. But after paying a few other leads, I can hire a caravan in a town not far from the Bright City. I plan to leave an encoded voice message to go live on Victoria's wristband 20 minutes after the ceremony. She'd be able to escape Marina and Roman's trap, and I'd be long gone. I go through the plan again, twisting and turning it over in my mind. I can't imagine betraying Victoria. I can't justify many of her actions but whatever Roman has planned it can't be good and I don't want any more blood on my hands. As I drift off to sleep, I feel satisfied with the plan. I'll keep playing along with Marina and Roman until I don't need them any longer. I'm coming home Katherine, and I'm going to find out why my father ordered your murder.

The next day, while playing chess with Victoria, I don't hear Marina come in before she tackles me. I crash against the hard floor and feel the sting of cold steel against my throat. Her eyes are distant and empty.

"Marina," Victoria yells, pulling her off me by her shirt.

"Tell her what you have, you little traitor," Marina screams back at me.

"I…don't…"

"What do you have, Abigail?" Victoria asks, her voice melting into her negotiating tone.

"I…well…I have information."

"Really," Victoria says, sitting across from me, waving the staff out of the room.

"It's here," I say, holding up the disc.

Marina lunges towards me but I sidestep her, and she

lands in a pile near Victoria's feet.

"That's mine, bitch!"

"No, it's not," I say, gathering my confidence.

"Hold on! Anything in my house is mine, first, if I deem it worthy to be mine. You know the rules, Marina."

"You don't understand; she tricked me out of this information," Marina pleads.

"Oh? And how did she do that?"

"We traded. That disc for the piece of information I gave you last week regarding the Chancellor's movements on induction day."

"Hmmm…so how did she trick you? Fair trade. One piece of information for another."

"Not fair. I found out that Abby had Maury encode the disc with something much more valuable."

Victoria's throaty laugh fills the room as she stands up and moves closer to me.

"Sounds perfectly fair to me. What have I always told you about data discs, Marina."

"Encode, decode, encrypt, decipher," I interrupt.

"Yes, sounds like someone was listening to me."

"I could have used that to purchase the last bond on my name," Marina yells.

BRIGHT CITY

Victoria turns to her, her jade eyes going cold. Then I realize Marina needs to have an excuse to hate Victoria. I pray Victoria won't give her a reason.

"Your bond," Victoria's voice is cold and distant, "that is what this is about."

"It's no secret; I want to start my Brokerage."

"It hasn't been a secret, you're right. But unfortunately, you're not there tonight."

Marina pushes her way past me and slams our shared bedroom door behind her. The staff returns to the living room, and I wait. I know Victoria is gathering herself, waiting for me to approach her. But I've learned; she respects steely resolve. The patient I am, the more she will think I plan on using the information as a bond trade as well. Or worse, trade with a competitor. I fall into my role, serving her when asked. Making small info trades on my DAT. She'd told me earlier in the day that the markets would be more aggressive during the festival while people attempt to amass enough money to take the rest of the year off. Even at the small exchanges, I am doing well; I notice her smile tightens at each beep on my wristband. I can tell she loves that I embraced her skills, but, at the same time, the scene with Marina makes her cautious.

An hour later when Marina leaves the house with only grudgingly saying that she has an Exchange, Victoria coolly dismisses the staff behind her. I can tell that the always self-possessed Victoria is working out the angles in her head. She is desperate to know what information, I have, but she is cautious, always calculating the most likely result.

"Abigail, leave the markets alone," she grumbles as a succession of beeps emanates from my band.

"Sorry, I suppose I should have turned the volume down," I say.

"No, no. I shouldn't snap," Victoria says, slipping into a pink and green flowered silk gown.

"The scene with Marina and me. She's just...desperate. That's all."

"So she's not correct. The information you have isn't worth as much as she thinks," Victoria asks.

"Well, it's not."

"Ah, well, inexperienced Brokers have a hard time gauging..."

"It's worth more," I interject.

Victoria abruptly stops tightening the belt on her robe. I've never seen her without words. At this moment she doesn't move. She's left herself vulnerable. I move in for the strike.

"But you'll forgive me if I ask for something in exchange."

"Of course, you'll wager for your bond."

"I don't want my bond."

"Well," Victoria sighs, picking a grape from the basket

on the table between us, "what is it you want?"

"I want to be your *Chusei*," I say, holding out the disc.

The look on Victoria's face says everything. She's been looking for this type of loyalty; complete fealty to her and her cause. She's told us more than once that as long as we were bondwomen, she keeps us at arm's length. Because if we managed to buy our bond, we'd be competition. But she's also insinuated the other Brokerages, which have *Chusei* have an advantage. The Apex and Uppers see them as more stable. And it's only been through her skills that she's maintained her status. This commitment of fealty, to become *Chusei*, means that I would be willing to give up everything to be loyal to her. My bond is hers for life. And also, she sees the long game and what that means for her ambitions and desires. She's well known, but she wants to be legendary.

"You know what you're saying? If this information is as good as you believe, you will never see the Colony again. You cannot leave the Bright City unless I say so. And if you do, you will be executed. *Chusei* is not a thing we just throw around."

"I know."

"Let me see the disc," she says.

"Before I give this to you…"

"Ahhh I knew there was a catch."

"If this information is not worth my pledge now, promise me that you will make me *Chusei* once I pay my bond."

"*Chusei* no matter what?"

I nod. Too afraid my voice will break if I speak.

"Intriguing."

I hand her the disc. She slips it into the data drive next to the screen in the living room. I watch the false information come alive on the screen. This information is minor; the names of the inductees to Kaiji. This information is an easy trade. What makes it valuable is each inductee's market account numbers are listed too. Any other Broker would think this was worth its weight in credits. Numerical strings connect silent sponsors to their market numbers. The Chancellor sponsored two of the Kaiji, specifically the special promotion.

"Interesting...for another Broker," Victoria says.

"I knew you probably had this information after Roman's visit."

"Smart," Victoria says.

"Do you see the key?"

Victoria turns back to the screen and taps the edge then spreads her index finger and thumb apart to open what looks like a lock. She slides her hands across the screen quickly gathering the pieces of the key from the market numbers. When she assembles the virtual key, she pauses before sliding it to the lock.

"Tell me why you want to be *Chusei*. Honestly."

"I don't."

"You don't what?"

"I don't *want* to be *Chusei*."

"I didn't think so."

"I *need* to be *Chusei*."

"Interesting."

"It's stupid, but I miss the Colony. My father exiled me. I have nothing. But with you, with Marina, this life…it's not anything I would have ever wanted but I…I want to have a family…like I did back home."

"This will be nothing like your home."

"I know. Because if I'm *Chusei*, we'll be loyal to each other."

She turns towards the screen and slides the virtual key into the lock. The images burst apart and reveal a recent picture of Ambassador Snyder. He looks older for his years. No longer fresh-faced and privileged. He looks like his time in the Outlands made him wiser and deadlier. The information Marina uncovered is thorough. The rumor is he was being passed among some Outlander gangs over a month before being traded to Knute tribesmen for fresh supplies. It wasn't long before they realized they had a Bright City ambassador and tried to make deals. But even the Chancellor wasn't interested in his return. The Ambassador has a lot of scores to settle. Victoria is last on his list, but she is on his list. The crucial point is that he brought Cleary with him. And their passage back to the city is on Commander Russell's credits. The Ambassador and the Commander were making plans to stage a coup against the Chancellor. All of their embedded schemes displayed in the data: voice overlays, maps, direct chatter, credits, and dates. All of this treasonous information could be used to take them both down, and now it's in Victoria's possession. The irony of it all, a data disc, the words and deeds of traitors, and I am holding the evidence again.

"What you have here could have earned you freedom from me, the Bright City and an army to avenge your exile," Victoria says, removing the disc from the screen.

"That's good to know."

"And yet you chose to give it to me."

"Yes."

"Do you have copies?"

"A good *Chusei* would never have a copy of something to sell to another Broker," I said.

"No, a good *Chusei* would not," she says.

She circles me looking closely. One of her hands trails along my arm, then my back, then my waist. I try to stand still; I feel goosebumps rise on my skin, and my body heats up. My stomach twists as her hand caresses my stomach. She steps closer and breathes in my scent. I try not to move. I beg my body not to betray me.

"It's no secret," Victoria whispers, "that I've wanted to fuck you for a very long time."

BRIGHT CITY

"Why haven't you tried?"

"I didn't think I could trust you."

"What makes you think you can trust me now?"

"Now, I don't care."

She pulls me into her arms. Her lips devour mine. Her kisses are hungry and sweet. I step back. She looks hungry. Her heavy-lidded green eyes turn dark. She doesn't let me go far. She holds onto my wrist, refusing to let go.

"I don't know," I say.

"Trust me," she says, pulling me to her bedroom.

I've been in her room dozens of times. Fantasized about being splayed on her bed with her over me, kissing me. I've imagined her stepping out of her tub, her body glistening with water, but this moment is too real. I lay down, and she climbs on top of me. I let her pull my shirt over my head, and I moan as she takes each nipple between her teeth; sucking and licking gently. I run my hands through her thick auburn hair. She pulls my pants and underwear off at the same time as her lips move further down my chest to my stomach and then my thighs. I gasp as she puts two fingers inside me. I tense around her long fingers as she tenderly moves them in and out of me. She sucks on my tongue then licks my earlobe. She holds me close to her as I rock with the rhythm of her fingers.

"You are beautiful," Victoria whispers.

I push her deeper inside me. I drift into my fantasies of escaping away from the Bright City, but she is beside me. Just us two in a tent in the Outlands. Just us away from it all, next to the ocean. Our bodies entwined, her cool breath against my skin. Our lips crushed together as the waves crash outside the thin walls of our home. I ride through that fantasy as my body fluctuates between hot and cold; my skin drips with sweat as she pushes into me and licks the dripping salt from my neck.

"Oh God," I cry out as my body spasms.

My body is electric. We are different together. We fit. I am hungry for her, starving for more.

Victoria smiles as her head disappears between my thighs, and I yelp as her tongue licks each and every fold. She holds my hips so that I can't move away and soon I'm grasping her head pushing her closer.

"Please don't stop," I moan.

I bask in this moment. The scent of her sweet musk, the feel of her lips and tongue between my legs, the grasp of her hands holding my hips; guiding me as she makes love to me.

When Victoria pushes her fingers inside me again, I gasp. She presses her lips to mine; sucks on my tongue and bites my lips. We rock together; back and forth, her fingers slip in and out of me.

"You are beautiful," she breathes into my ear.

She grasps my waist with one arm and pulls me closer as her fingers dive deeper. I don't want this to end. I need it not to end. But my body doesn't listen. I feel a tremor between my legs chase its way up to my stomach. I grip her tightly as my body shakes with pleasure.

"I love you," I cry out at the height of my ecstasy.

I lay in Victoria's arms as the weight of what happened crashes into me. I push my plans to betray her out of my mind. I try to be in this moment with her.

"You love me, huh?" Victoria chuckles.

"Who knows," I say, pulling the sheet up around my chest.

"I mean, didn't you hate me not too long ago?"

"Yes. Maybe I still do."

"No, I'm pretty sure after what we just did you love me."

"God, you're arrogant," I say moving away from her.

She laughs and pulls me back in her arms, kissing my neck and placing my hand between her legs. She moans as she moves my hand gently up and down.

"Mmmm, I may be arrogant, but I know when I want something I go get it."

She pushes me back on the bed so that she can lie on top of me. She pushes one of her legs between mine and rests on her elbows above me. Her lips are swollen and red. I resist the urge to suck on them.

"You want me," I ask.

"I have you," she says.

"For now."

She kisses me; letting her tongue explore my mouth. I can taste myself on her lips. She pulls me into her arms; running her hands through my tangled hair. Our hands explore each other's bodies. She is just as soft as I thought she'd be. I notice the raised slick scars in odd places and a tawny birthmark in the shape of a cloud on her hip. We kiss until she pulls away; wiping her mouth with the back of her hand; she shakes her red mane then sits up and away from me. I long for the warmth of her body against mine.

"Let's take a bath," she offers.

"Why'd you pull away? Are you afraid?"

"Deathly," she says, pulling me up and towards the bathroom.

"Me too," I whisper.

When she clamps the silver and wood ring around my right finger a week later, I wince because it hurts but also because I realize I've sold out Victoria. My heart hurts even if it was for my freedom. I became a traitor, and in my heart I know I'll have to pay the price.

CHAPTER TWENTY-THREE

৵•৶

I **MOVE INTO VICTORIA'S BEDROOM AFTER** our first night together. The next day she brought in tailors to ensure I had any clothing I wanted. I settled on mirroring her daily uniform; leather pants, calf-high boots, burgundy silk shirts and black leather trenches. She approved. When Marina came home, I tried to talk to her. But she brushed me off. Later in the week when we were in Roman's club she told me that she was just playing a game with Victoria. I don't believe her. I'm not so sure about much of anything right now. The past couple of months has been amazing. More than I expected it to be. More than I wanted it to be. I want to be bitter. I want to hate Victoria. I want to feel trapped. But now I feel free. I move through the Bright City now as Victoria's right hand. People smile in my direction, stop me to chat and give me information to gain our favor. And there are days when I forget about the Kingdom and even Katherine. I hate myself for those moments.

Victoria makes this forgetfulness easy. She showers me with clothing, attention, and affection. She opens up more. One night, in bed, she tells me about her mother. A pale raven-haired beauty who had been a doctor for a small town that survived The Fall. I sometimes wonder if she is playing me. I can't trust anyone. I tell myself this whenever I find myself slipping under her spell. She's a master manipulator. There's no one as good at keeping secrets as she is.

I can choose my clients now. And Victoria pushes me to be extra selective. Prolets whisper about our Brokerage. In the past month, I spent some time with Senator Riley and one evening with a young *Tyro*, a friend of Roman's. Both were lucrative in their own ways; Senator Riley for the Exchange and the *Tyro* for some information on Roman. I realize Roman's circle may be small, but it is not as tight as he thinks it is. I'm happy I've worked out another plan to get away from Roman and Marina. My role in our Brokerage has changed. Victoria and Marina have grown more distant. I am the wedge between them. Now, whenever Marina brings home information, I judge its worth. There have been tense moments between us, but I keep telling myself it's all worth it to make my plan work.

Power is thrilling. In my few moments alone, I think about Katherine and what she would say about this. Would the power rush I'm experiencing confirm her worst thoughts of me? Am I just as eager for control as she believed me to be? Sometimes, when I'm roaming the Bright City, I think about my last interaction with her. I haven't about it for over a year. It came to me one night after Victoria fell asleep. I dreamt of that room again. Cold and uninviting. Back then it didn't seem different from any other place. Now, it's the last place I want to be. Katherine is sitting across from me, examining me, in the way she sometimes would. Her hazel eyes were searching my face for some sign of compassion. This time though she's not searching for compassion, but for the part of my face, she wants to ruin. I'm trying to explain to her how I got caught up with Victoria, that I'm doing this for us. And just as the punch connects with my jaw I wake up. She wouldn't approve of this relationship. Even if I explained that it's so I could escape. I hear her voice sneering the words, "Sure you are, Vice Regent" at me as her eyes burn a hole through my soul. I cannot damn myself to this. I'm starting to doubt my ability to resist.

But I'm important again. I never realized how addicting it is, knowing that you could make change happen with just a word. As a *Chusei*, I have the freedom to wear what I want. The only exception is I must I wear my Brokerage armband. In other words, wherever I go I am marked, exposed.

Tonight, Tinka is supposed to escort me to an Upper party; the first one of the upcoming Lunar Festival. According to the rules, it's her responsibility as the senior *Chusei* to escort me to a large social event as a way of introducing me to the Uppers. Now here we are at the social event of the season, and she's suspiciously absent.

I maintain my composure and try to imagine what Victoria would do. She'd find Tinka and make her pay, I think. I look around and see lots of familiar faces. Roman and Cleary are there. Roman is entertaining two Upper women with matching blonde hair and eager smiles. I've seen them several times in Prolet clubs. Cleary looks angry, as usual. When he spots me, his eyes narrow and his full lips shrink to a fine line. More than once he's told me that he hates me. He can't forgive Victoria for hurting his father's standing with the clans, and because I'm her lover, he can't forgive me either. It's all good; I don't trust him either. I can't think about him tonight. He's a problem for another day, a problem I have to solve quickly if I want to maintain my alternate escape plan.

I take a glass of champagne from a passing server and make my way towards some brightly dressed *Chusei*. No matter what party they attend, they're either with their clients or by the booze, gossiping.

"Good evening, everyone," I say, giving the *Chusei* bow; a slight twist of the waist to the right while also slightly leaning your left shoulder to the right.

"Well, at least you got the bow right," *Chusei* Erik, snips.

Victoria would be proud. She had her team dress me in an all black wide-legged jumpsuit that cinches tight at the waist. With the only pop of color being my lips and armband, maroon for the armband; a shade lighter for my lips.

"Good you noticed Erik. Tinka was supposed to bring me, but I hear she's with Ambassador Tracey. I hope it wasn't presumptuous for me to attend anyway. It's possible she forgot. My Danna says the beginning of the Lunar celebrations can be chaotic."

"She didn't forget," *Chusei* Becca, speaks up.

"Then she willfully ignored her duties? I can't believe she would do such a thing," I say, feigning surprise.

"No…it's…just…"

BRIGHT CITY

"I completely understand. She doesn't have time for someone like me. I'm merely trying to follow in her footsteps."

"Ha," Erik sneers, toasting me with a nod towards Tinka, "I'm sure she'd love to speak to you."

I approach her while smiling and greeting various members of The Apex. Just as I step up beside Tinka, I catch Ambassador Tracey's eye. And how could I not? The jumpsuit I'm wearing has a deep V-neck that hints at the lace and leather bra I'm wearing underneath. Victoria said he is a leather fiend. More importantly, he's obsessed with the hidden. I can see that Tinka didn't get that memo. She's here in all her finest leather, perfect for someone other than Ambassador Tracey, someone who would want her to show that ensemble off in the bedroom.

"*Chusei* Tinka, I thought we had a date," I say as I step between her and Ambassador Tracey.

"Oh, *Chusei* Abigail. I didn't know you ranked an invitation to this event."

"Omni Brokerage is invited to every event of the Lunar Festival," I say, "but I beg your forgiveness. I clearly must have caused you disgrace as you decided not to escort me to this event."

I slip to my knees and hear Ambassador Tracey try to clear his throat.

"Get up," Tinka sneers.

"Do I deserve to stand in front of you?"

"Ugh, no but get up. You're causing a scene."

I reach out my hand and Ambassador Tracey pulls me to my feet. I "accidentally" stumble into his chest.

"Pardon me, Ambassador. Forgive me for interrupting your Exchange."

"It's no problem at all," he says, pushing a curled tendril away from my face.

"Thank you, excuse me."

I bow to Tinka and slowly move back through the crowd and over to Roman and Cleary.

"Quite a game you're playing tonight," Roman laughs, passing me an electronic cigarette.

Cleary turns up his nose at me before being pulled off to dance by one of the older Upper women.

"It's all a game right? To get to the end, we have to play the hand we're dealt," I say.

"True. But I'd hate to see you at my table," Roman says, nodding in Ambassador Tracey's direction.

Ambassador Tracey in his ebony majesty is striding in our direction. I look past him at Tinka. She is all frowns. She catches my eye, drags her finger across her throat, and then stomps towards the door.

"Abigail is it?" Ambassador Tracey asks before he kisses my hand.

BRIGHT CITY

"Play to win," Roman says under his breath before he blends into the crowd.

I stand in the shower, rinsing Ambassador Tracey off my body. I hate this part. Surprisingly, Ambassador Tracey was more than forthcoming with information. But then again, not so surprising, I paid plenty for the data. I gently rub soap over my bruised butt and thighs. I say, no tears, but my eyes don't listen. I lean against the steamy wall and let them fall. I've come a long way from Vice Regent. Vice Regent. Who would believe that now? I see a partial reflection of myself in the glass door; the eyeliner drips down my cheeks, my hair falls out of its intricate bun. I don't see myself anymore. I see the woman I've become. She's a stranger to me. Vice Regent Abigail would keep her word. She would not lie or betray anyone. She was good. This woman is desperate. And desperation is a drug.

"Abigail?" Victoria says from the bathroom doorway.

I sniff out a yes and turn away from the glass door of the shower. I feel her body against mine before I can turn around.

"I put the information from Ambassador Tracey in your DAT as soon as I got home. I'm sorry I woke you," I whisper.

"Fuck his information. What's wrong? What happened," she asks.

"Nothing. Nothing we didn't talk about before."

"No, I…" Victoria turns me towards her and her lips caress mine.

"What," I ask.

"I should trust you with everything. You've done nothing but prove to me that you could be trusted, and I sent you in there without knowing everything. I'm sorry," Victoria says. "What didn't I know," I ask.

"I knew Tinka was going to be a bitch. I knew because her *Danna* owes one of my clients a favor, and she can't keep her mouth shut."

"What's going on?"

"I'm going to destroy Zhou Brokerage. I have the money, the data, and the leverage. And Tinka was just a way to begin dismantling their status," she confesses.

"You used me and didn't tell me?"

"Yes, and I'm sorry. I know that as my *Chusei* you should be aware of all the information. I should have told you. I was just..."

"Just what? Afraid?"

"Maybe. I don't know. I'm so used to doing this on my own," Victoria says.

"You don't trust me," I say.

"I do. I do trust you."

I lean into her, and half listen while she whispers lusty confessions into my ear. I don't blame her for not trusting me. She shouldn't. But this seals it. I sacrificed myself for her, and she's begging me for forgiveness. I peek over her

BRIGHT CITY

shoulder at my reflection in the mirror; I lose myself in the woman staring back at me. Maybe I can find me again when I escape.

CHAPTER TWENTY-FOUR

ॐ•ॐ

THE BRIGHT RED, LILAC, AND yellow desert roses gleam against a dazzling shower of gold sunrays. I can smell the salty ocean and fish as our caravan speeds towards the wedding. I reread my invitation. It's made out of paper, so it's expensive. The silky insert with my name on it smells like jasmine. *Chusei* Abigail of the Omni Brokerage. It's been three months since I became *Chusei*. This wedding is the first time I've been outside of the Bright City. I adjust the burgundy armband and remind myself of my training. Listen, speak carefully, and maintain poise.

Victoria's laughter fills the noisy car, and I glance in her direction. Her escort is Kaiji Ambrose, a military specialist who just returned from accompanying an Ambassador to a city in the south. Victoria's wearing her favorite color, jade, with large silver hoops peeking from behind her tumble of red hair. I think about our conversation earlier today. This mission to make Tinka begin a descent into self-doubt disturbs me. I'm not a fan of

BRIGHT CITY

Tinka. I've come to find that no one is. In the time that I've been a *Chusei*, she has avoided me. The rivalry that Victoria has with the Zhou Brokerage is bigger than Tinka or me. Victoria sees Tinka as collateral damage.

There is plenty of laughter and excitement in our crowded speeding rail compartment. Our invitation onto the personal speed rail of Senator Ambrose for his daughter's wedding came from the Senator himself. A gift for the Brokerage after my evening with him and his wife. The Travellers clan tumbling team that I met in Knute has joined us, Victoria's present to the couple for the reception. The tumblers drink and joke with one another attempting to entertain everyone with a game called, "One Up." They try to best one another by telling fantastic stories about everything from their prowess in bed to the journeys they've taken around the Outlands.

"Five miles to the Circle Ranch; we will be passing through several security gates so be aware," the driver announces over an intercom.

We pass by the first white stakes with colorful ribbons blowing in the hot wind, and ahead I can see a trail of black cars snaking towards an estate set on top of a lush green hill.

"Grass," I whisper.

"He supposedly has it flown in from the east coast. He has an army of gardeners," Marina says.

"He doesn't live in the city? Isn't he afraid of clans destroying this place?"

"You'll see why he's not afraid."

Armed guards occupy the sides of the first gates to the estate. Others roam around the cars using mirrors to look underneath the carriages. Guards search the compartments of our speeding rail then run items through a machine that scans for potential explosives and other dangers. Two of the tumblers produce contracts showing that they would absorb all costs and are subject to life imprisonment if something happened to any guest while they are doing their fire-breathing act. Finally, we pass through body scanners at the entrance to the residential compound. Both Victoria and I have individual scans because of the metal in our bustiers.

The wedding is brief. No more than 20 minutes. For Uppers in the Bright City, it's all about the party and games. I remember my manners as we move through the reception line at the entrance to the lushly decorated dining hall. Two kisses for the husband and one for the bride, smile, discreetly pass the bride a token from our Brokerage, a gold coin with a maroon circle at its center embossed with our Panther sigil. She may use it for one free, no strings attached Exchange. I didn't have to ask Victoria if this was an acceptable gift. I know it is. We know what every other Brokerage is giving to the couple. None of them could afford the unlimited possibilities that type of gift could provide.

The building is awash in white. Green vines with white flowers dripping from every stem cascade across the ceiling and walls making the inside of the building feel like we are walking through an enchanted forest. Guests enjoy games in nearly every corner. Cheers and groans rise and fall amongst the crowds, occasionally drowning out the thumping music pulsating from speakers at the back of the room.

BRIGHT CITY

We find our assigned sofas along the wall near the center of the lounge. Servants quickly bring us wine and food while admirers swarm our group. I relax, getting into the spirit of the excitement and joy of the celebration.

"The other *Chusei* have arrived," Victoria says, "Marina, take Abigail over to them."

Marina pulls me towards the brightly dressed crowd of young men and women.

"Now entering the lion's den," I murmur.

"You've been trained to deal with these assholes. Remember, screw them. Victoria wants to destroy Tinka. This is her final test of loyalty. We keep moving forward you only have a few more weeks, and this is all over. Do what you gotta do."

I make eye contact with Tinka as we approach the group. She cuts her violet eyes in my direction and whispers to Siobhan who flips her braids and turns back towards the game they're standing around.

"Shit, this is not going to be pretty," I say.

"Don't worry; I have it on good authority that Tinka is going to be in rare form tonight. She saw you give the bride that coin. She'll want to know whose idea it was. I suggest being coy about it. And of course, since you were able to wrangle Ambassador Tracey from her she's been losing her mind."

"So I'm walking into a hornet's nest."

"Hornet's nest, lion's den. It's all the same, isn't it? Besides, they think you're a creative and manipulative *Chusei* who will stop at nothing to succeed. And they still want to know how you got Victoria to accept you as *Chusei* before me. Word on the street is that you had some information that was big, juicy and volatile. Remember, discretion is essential."

"Well, hello Marina. Abigail," a lanky young man with piercing silver eyes, says a bit too loudly.

"Hello *Chusei* Nix," Marina says.

"Abigail, you look delicious," Nix says, running a hand quickly over my arm.

"*Chusei* Abigail, I have an errand, enjoy yourself," Marina says with a smirk.

"Do you know this game," Siobhan asks.

"No, looks fascinating," I lie. I know the game. I've played it with Victoria every night.

"It's called Paduk," Nix says, pulling me closer to the action.

"Looks fun," I say.

"Fun?" Tinka scoffs.

"You should play her Tinks," an ebony-skinned girl with bright blonde dreads says.

"I'd love to learn from you, *Chusei* Tinka," I say, kissing her hand. It's a submissive gesture I knew would

BRIGHT CITY

throw off and annoy Tinka.

Tinka whistles and the two *Chusei* playing get up in the middle of their game. We sit at opposite ends of a small wooden table while we place tiny round stones, along a grid burned into the table. She selects the white stones, and I use the black. Tinka explains the object is to place the stones on an empty spot on the grid. Stones must be aligned in chains to remain on the board. If one player's chain breaks the other player's then that player gets to keep the stones. The game moves rapidly. I make my first moves. She plays aggressively. She moves her chains around the board so that she nearly surrounds mine. Soon, we have a crowd around us cheering. Several times I see holes in her strategy, but I avoid poking them.

"And they say you're cunning," Tinka sneers.

"Who says such a thing?" I ask, scooping up three of her perimeter stones.

"No one who should be believed," she responds picking up six of my stones.

I smile. In four moves, I can win. I don't. I let Tinka move in for the kill. When she wins, the other *Chusei* surround her praising her, giving her compliments.

I back away and blend into the crowd. I spend most of the evening talking with some of the men Victoria told me I should watch earlier. I manage to dance for hours and drink much more than I should have. Right before dawn, I explore the garden. It's lit with hundreds of torches. In the dark corners, shadows of couples making out dance along the ivy-covered walls. I walk towards the edge of the garden and lean on the cool metal railing.

"You think you're so smart."

I don't turn towards Tinka. I take a deep drink of warm mulled cider.

"You are not special. I've seen young *Chusei* like you. Thinking you can become a *Danna* by dropping a sweet word or sleeping with an Ambassador."

"I have no plans to be a *Danna*," I say.

"Every *Chusei* wants to own their a Brokerage. Don't be coy."

I don't turn around. I wait for Tinka to come to me. After a few minutes, she stands beside me, placing her back against the railing.

"I don't want a Brokerage," I say staring into her heavy-lidded eyes.

"You are a liar."

"I don't want a Brokerage, but I do have plans."

"Well spit it out, what do you want."

I turn to face her. I lean into her. She smells like warm vanilla.

"I will be the greatest *Chusei* the Bright City has ever seen," I whisper in her ear.

She pushes me away from her, a scowl creasing her face. I grin and raise my mug in her direction.

"Stay out of my way," she growls.

"*Chusei* Tinka, how could you be threatened by someone who couldn't even beat you at Paduk?"

"I knew you weren't playing at your best; you know that don't you? I thrashed you on that board to make a point," Tinka says.

"And what point was that?"

"That I can crush you."

"You owe me for not destroying your reputation," I say.

"Stay out of my way, you arrogant bitch," she spits.

"Of course, as long as you stay out of mine."

Victoria steps out of one of the dark corners slowly clapping. She takes my cup and finishes my cider.

"Now you have her shaken," Victoria says.

"What do you think she'll do?"

"She'll start a campaign against you. She'll try to get all the other *Chusei* to ignore you. And while some of them are sheep a few of the key ones will wonder why she's so worried about you."

"Why do you want me to take her clients? All of this seems a bit beneath you."

"Oh darling, think like a *Danna*."

"She's trying to purchase The Zhou Brokerage firm."

"Good girl," Victoria says, kissing my exposed shoulder.

"If she's put her bid in, her Danna must want her to own it."

"No, she hasn't submitted her proposal yet. She's waiting for the price to go down. She's driving the price down. She's been placing information with different sources. She just hasn't realized those are my sources. And, of course, that information is priceless."

"If you buy the Brokerage, what will you do with her? She'll be superior to me."

"No, not her. I have plans for her," Victoria says.

"The same plans you had for me when you kidnapped me?" I ask.

"No, different plans. Now don't you worry about Tinka, you're my number one. I promise you."

Victoria pulls me into an embrace. We watch the sun rise over the distant desert hills, making the clouds above them gold and red puffs. I lean into her arms and realize in two weeks this will be over. I will be in Section Two. She will lose her Brokerage. She will be the collateral damage that I leave behind. For the first time since I began this journey, I hate myself.

CHAPTER TWENTY-FIVE

ৡ•ঌ

"Be impressed, but not overly so," Victoria says with a nudge.I've seen places like this before. My mother had a picture book of fairy tales she read to me at night. My father thought the whole process was nonsense. He wanted to read me history books. My mother insisted. Still, the pictures of 17th-century ballrooms pale next to the real thing.

The room reminds me of icing on a cake, the bright cream-colored walls, the long tables with ivory colored tablecloths, and the scent of vanilla cream filling the massive space. Elaborate flower centerpieces surround gold-rimmed china, polished silverware and sparkling goblets. The mellow and soothing music from the band performing on an elevated stage feels like a seduction. In the middle of all of this white, I feel nearly naked in a black-leather corseted dress. Black straps cover my legs; a long train extends from the back of my metallic corset. Vinyl sleeves connected to a high leather collar cover my arms. I touch the newly-shaved sides of my hair and take a full step into the ballroom. I miss my jeans.

I drift through the room smiling and laughing, pretending that my heart isn't thumping out of my chest. Tonight I am abandoning Victoria. I am running away from her, and I hurt so deeply I can barely stand it. Part of me wants to stay. Part of me can't stand the thought that after tonight I will be far away from the Bright City, and Victoria's ambition will crush her. "I'm sorry love," I think as I watch her laugh and chat with various Uppers. She is beautiful. I reminisce on last night; her body entwined with mine. Her throaty laughter when I nuzzled her neck. Her moans when I kissed her between her thighs. Her fingers deep in me. I'm sorry Katherine, but Victoria is my greatest regret. I accidentally screwed up with you, but I'm intentionally screwing Victoria. I chat with two of my clients who flirt with me shamelessly. I demure, blush and giggle. The game.

After the wedding, there was no separating Victoria and me. Many moments when we made love I forgot about running away. But then I'd see Marina, and it would all come flooding back. I remind myself, I am supposed to betray Victoria even though I'm falling in love. Sometimes, Marina is subservient and sometimes distant. She's playing the heartbroken servant, and I'm supposed to be the haughty victor. Her cruelty in public makes it easy to be mean to her. In private she chats happily about taking Victoria down. I laugh with her, but inside I'm dying. Playing two games is ruining me. I can barely look in a mirror. I don't see me anymore. This girl, this woman, is different, darker, more dangerous.

I spot Tinka as I chat with a Kaiji soldier and his Tyro. The mighty have fallen. A week after the wedding Victoria dismantled Zhou Brokerage. Tinka moved on to Pascal

Brokerage, but the move destroyed her ranking the *Chusei*. I raise my glass in her direction, and she turns her back. I get it. I ruined her. But maybe she'll take some joy in Victoria's downfall. Maybe they'll console one another. I doubt it, but I hope for some redemption in all of this.

When I spot Roman walking towards me, I extract myself from the clients and meet Roman half way. I look past Roman and nod at Cleary. He looks miserable, he cuts his eyes at me, and his lips curl into a scowl. I give him a smile and a wink. I turn my back to Cleary and lean into Roman.

"I'm nervous. What if this doesn't work? If Victoria finds out about my escape before I can get out of the city, I'm going to prison."

"Abby, no need to be nervous. Our plan will work. Now, I have to take you to your date for the evening."

As we pass through the throngs of people, I catch snippets of conversations here and there. I find myself making mental notes. I swipe my fingers across my wristband to grab the chatter. I consider deleting it from my band, but I don't. Maybe I can use these to Exchange with Marina or Roman or both. My gut twists when I see Victoria across the room chatting with Maury. He looks spiffy. Marina was right; he cleans up well.

"Kaiji Roman, it looks like you have abandoned your post," a familiar voice comes from behind us. I feel Roman's hand stiffen around my wrist, and we turn to face Ambassador Snyder.

"No, sir. I am just taking *Chusei* Abigail to the sitting room to meet her escort for the evening."

"*Chusei*? Ah, you were just a lowly *dojin* when we last met. *Dojin*...a slut."

"And you were so kind, before you left the Bright City," I reply.

"Yes, I should thank your *Danna* for that trip."

"She would be most happy to see you, Ambassador Snyder. I'm sure she'd love to hear all about your trip to the Outlands."

"I'm sure she doesn't need any updates."

"Six months away from the creature comforts of home, traveling with gangs and then bringing back a young man for training in the Kaiji. Sounds like an adventure."

"Excuse me, Ambassador Snyder I must take *Chusei* Abigail to the sitting room," Roman interrupted.

"You'll go when I say."

"Careful Ambassador."

I hit a nerve. Ambassador Snyder's grip on my arm tightens as he pulls me close to his chest, a deadly smile creasing his lips. I look around us. No one is watching. Everyone is ignoring us. He is dangerously close to losing his status, and tonight, the night when fortunes rise and fall, he realizes he's on the precipice. Unlike most of the other Uppers, he's seen the truth of having nothing. The reports of his time in the Outlands were detailed and painful to read. He'd been passed around to several clans. There was a blurred image of him dressed in a silky dressing gown. He looked bruised and battered. The medical reports revealed tears and lacerations over most of his body. But Saul had been kind to him...for a price. Now I understand why he joined with his nemesis to overthrow the Chancellor. He is desperate.

"*Tyro* Cleary, please take Abigail to meet her sponsor for the evening. I should talk to Ambassador Snyder," Roman says, pushing me towards Cleary.

"Yes, run along *dojin*. You don't want to leave your *sponsor* waiting," Ambassador Snyder snarls at me.

Cleary grabs my arm just a bit tighter than necessary, and we glide through the guests who ignore us. My stomach tightens as we approach the curtained area that cordons me off from the ballroom. Before I enter the room, I look behind me to find Victoria. I want to see her for the last time. The crowd shifts and I see her red mane, and I swear I hear her lush laugh. I'll miss her.

I walk deeper into the room. It's sumptuous, draped mostly in purple and gold. There are large puffy couches pushed against the walls, and the lamps create warm, dim lighting. In the center of the room is a fake rock campfire but the smoke coming out of the flickering cloth flames fills the room with a delicious vanilla scent. Cleary paces in front of the entrance. He pulls off his hood and runs his hands through his longish hair. It's grown since we last saw each other.

"Back in a tent together," I joke.

He glares at me.

"Well, say something," I say.

"Something."

"Funny," I say, and then flop on the nearest couch. The leather corset I'm laced into pinches my ribs.

"You look different," he says.

"So do you."

"So this is how Victoria has you. All dolled up. Entertaining clients?"

"Who told you that?" I ask.

"Roman...Ambassador Snyder...and I can see that you're a high-class version of the women that come to our town once a month."

"I'm not like that," I say.

"Well, then what are you?"

"Why do you care? Your father, the one you're so interested in defending, was gonna use me like those women who come to your town."

"Yeah, of course, that's what a *mole* would think."

"Cut it out with that *mole* shit."

"Ambassador Snyder is going to kill you and Victoria."

"He thinks he is."

BRIGHT CITY

"You're an asshole; you know that," he says, pulling off his long gray hooded robe.

"I've heard that."

"You think Victoria is going to protect you? She's a mercenary. My father uses her to steal and murder and enslave. You're just one prize."

"Yeah, the funny thing is I know all this. Tell me something I don't know."

"I'm taking you back to Knute. We have a ceremony."

"A ceremony?" I ask.

"Yeah," he shifted from foot to foot, "you gotta marry me."

"Oh hell no!"

"Yeah. Hell yes. You'll do it because it'll save your skin."

"No damn way!"

"Listen to me. The only reason you're safe now is because of me. Ambassador Snyder has plans for this place, and we need to get out of here before he makes them happen."

"Plans?" I sit up, peering at Cleary in the dim light. How could he know about the plan to overthrow the Chancellor?

"He's going to take down the Chancellor, but his

personal vendetta is against Victoria."

"Wait. How do you know all this?"

"My father was pissed with Victoria. She shamed him. After she caused that ruckus, the clans withdrew most of their trades. The only way he can regain his standing if he can prove she's dead, and I bring you back."

"Ambassador Snyder promised that he would murder Victoria," I say, seeing the pieces slide into place.

"My father wasn't thinking straight. He was trying to control his clan. Win his standing back among the leaders. He thought saving this guy would benefit him."

"How am I supposed to trust what you're saying?"

"You don't believe me. Go with your gut. Do you think that if some city boy like Snyder got shipped to the Outlands that he would have survived even a day?"

I twisted his words in my mind. How could that be if not for someone on the inside controlling this whole charade?

"So you're gonna take me back. What about Victoria?"

"Let Snyder deal with her. She doesn't matter to me."

"So your father doesn't want to have personal retribution?"

"Bringing you back to Knute is enough for him."

"How are we gonna get out? I'm known here. And I'm

Victoria's *Chusei*."

"No one gives a shit about this City and its rankings and foo-foo. Besides this place is gonna crumble under Ambassador Snyder."

I shake my head and wonder what's taking Roman so long to bring my client. The faster we can push our plan forward, the faster I can escape. I'm not going back to Knute. Not with Cleary, not ever. I look up when the music in the ballroom dies down. Thunderous clapping punctuates a brief silence. An electronic squeal pierces the clapping, and then a man's voice echoes through the chamber.

"Welcome citizens to the Lunar Festival!"

The voice continues giving the history of the Lunar Festival in conjunction with the elevation of the Kaiji. The voice adds a brief history of the Bright City. Once a small port town in The Before, it became a stronghold during the war. Unlike most cities, it flourished. And for over a century it still stands. Cheers fill the hall. I move closer to the curtains as Cleary slips his robe back over his shoulders.

"You have to stay here," Cleary says.

"Where are you going?"

"To be confirmed."

"You're going to be Kaiji?"

"Get the black cloak and be able to move around the city without a problem? Of course, I'm getting it. Now if that *client* comes, don't let him take you away from here.

I'll dispose of him when I get back," Cleary says.

"What if I'm not here when you get back?"

"You'll be here. And if not, I'll hunt you down."

I grasp his hand before he parts the curtains. I want to tell him that I won't be here. That he can hunt me down, but I'm not sticking around. I want to tell him that the life he thinks we'll have won't come true, and I want to tell him that he made a mistake coming here. He'll be trapped. I don't say anything. His eyes soften, and he pushes through the curtain. That's when I hear the boom.

CHAPTER TWENTY-SIX

ॐ•ॐ

DOUGIE, THE BODYGUARD FROM the brothel, is leaning over me padding my forehead with a damp cloth. I hear Marina shouting at people around us; giving orders. I try to open my eyes but the light in the room stabs my pupils, and I snap my eyes shut.

"What the hell," I croak; through my dry throat, trying to push Dougie's hand away.

"She's awake," he yells out.

"Bring the volume down, will you?" I say touching my fingertips to my temples.

"Yeah, you'll be okay. Still, a smart ass," Marina says, pushing the man out of the way.

"Good, you're awake."

"We've established that."

"We gotta make moves if we want to get you out of the city."

"What the hell happened?"

"Bomb ripped apart the ballroom. You're lucky we found you. But it seems like we're not the only ones who wanted to ruin the Chancellor's big day," Marina says, shoving a bag of clothes at me.

"Where's Roman?"

"He had to get the rest of your supplies. He'll meet you beyond the gate."

"Is Cleary ok?" I ask.

"Concussion but he'll be fine," Dougie says.

"We have to take him with us," I say.

"He isn't part of our plan. Plus, he's knocked out."

"Dougie, you can carry him right?"

"No, Abigail, we gotta get out of here," Marina says, peeking out of the curtains.

"What about Victoria? Have you seen Victoria?" I ask.

"No, but she's resourceful. Now hurry up and get dressed."

"We have to see if she's ok," I say.

"Do you want to get out of here or do you want to see

if your jailer is ok? You have choices to make. Get ready,"
Marina snaps.

I pull on the clothes and throw my dress behind the
couch. Dougie lifts Cleary over his shoulder and starts out
in front of us making his way quickly to the entrance of the
ballroom. I'm numb. Above the ringing, in my ears, chaotic
screaming and shouting echo beyond the curtain. The scent
of burning flesh and hair seem to fill up the small space,
and I try not to gag.

"You ready?" Marina asks.

I nod and follow.

The ballroom reminds me of a picture I saw when we
studied The Fall. The day of the invasion, long before I was
born, caused devastation across the US. The invaders hit
both coasts at once. Due to a virus in the satellites, whole
city blocks were destroyed by drones. The picture was
black and white. But I remember even in my seventh year
class that I could envision the colors. Mr. Jansky explained
the incident in detail, but all I could do was stare at the
image on my desk. The bodies were everywhere. I
remember I could see a head and torso ripped apart, but the
elongated tendons spilling out of both parts seemed to
reach out to one another. I remember wanting to put the
body back together, knowing I couldn't. The image haunted
me for years. No one lived. No one survived. Everyone
died.

My mind snaps to Victoria. Where is she? Did she get
out? My heart pounds against my chest. I search the dead
for her auburn hair. I find myself tripping over bodies. I
fight back tears. I don't want Marina to see me worrying.

"C'mon," Marina snaps.

I force my eyes to focus on the reality in front of me.
The bloody mess that we are tramping through. I wonder
how either of them can see this destruction and not feel
anything.

We pick our way through the dead and wounded. As
we move quickly through the devastation we hear people
crying out for help. I slow down every couple of steps. I
recognize twisted faces, and my stomach lurches at the
sight of their mutilated bodies. At the ruined banquet table,
I see a pile of colorful clothes singed in the charred remains
of meat and sauces. As I get closer, I recognize, Tinka. Half
of her face is ripped from her skull, her blue eyes bulging
against her swelling skull. I turn away and trip over the
body in front of me.

"Come the fuck on Abby," Marina yells.

"Coming," I say.

I pull myself up. A hand clamps onto my ankle. I
scream.

"You'll never escape," grunts the man gripping me.

I can see his ring glinting against his nearly melted
skin. Ambassador Snyder. Behind me, I hear a click and
then his head explodes. When his hand goes lax I turn to
Marina, the gun smoking at her side, she points towards the
door. We run.

When we get out to the street, I suck in too much air
and stumble to the corner of a building. I throw up. The bile
stings my throat.

BRIGHT CITY

"We don't have time for this, Abby, let's go," Marina says as she runs ahead of me.

"She's right. We have to get you off the street and out of the city," says Dougie.

"I'm sorry."

"Don't be," Dougie passes me some water.

I take a swig, wipe my eyes and begin to run.

We zigzag through the crowded streets. I notice that news about the explosion hasn't reached the ground. People are still celebrating. We finally get to the maintenance doors Roman promised Marina would lead to a tunnel out of the city. Loud humming generators cover our splash into the tunnel. Dougie yanks the loose bars off the entrance, and we run into the darkness. Marina turns on her light tube, guiding us through the maze of underground sections.

"What happens when we get to the safe spot?" I ask.

"We have people waiting to give us supplies and your pass to Vector One," she replies.

"Vector One?"

"It's a city about 100 miles from here. You need a passport. But we have you covered," says Marina.

"Don't worry, we got this," Dougie says, patting my shoulder.

After an hour we get to a door. Dougie begins to drill into the bolts. I lean against the wall absently rubbing at the dust. I think about Victoria. Maybe when I get to Vector One, I can send for her. I'll hire some people to bring her to me.

"Hold the light closer, Mari," Dougie says.

I notice as the light passes the wall words under the half wiped wall.

"Re-Education Chamber," I whisper.

"What," Marina asks.

"The words next to the door," I nod at them.

"Yeah what about them?"

"Wait…this…can't…"

I step back and flash my lamp tube around the tunnels. I'd been so focused; I put my tracking skills aside. Now they are turned up. I backtrack a bit flashing the lamp tube around the high and low of the chamber. It's all around me. As we were walking, this all felt horribly familiar. But I ignored the feeling, chasing the possibility away from my mind. It couldn't be. And then I found it. Covered in webbing, scratched and dull but there. I pressed my hand to it. It glowed green. A few feet away I hear the airlock on the door depressurize and a long forgotten bulb above the handle blinks alive.

"Is this a Colony?"

CHAPTER TWENTY-SEVEN

৵•ৡ

B etrayal.

I never understood the word until last night. Marina
helped me betray Victoria, a woman that I love, a woman
whose loyalty I used. Now I sit here in this room with her. I
woke up a week ago in the same room that was once my
prison when I first arrived in the Bright City. At first, I was
alone, but I could hear noises beyond my door. I spent
hours yelling, kicking the door. After what seemed like
days two Kaiji threw Victoria in the room with me. I used
the remaining water the guards brought every morning to
clean her battered semi-conscious body. She hasn't spoken
since she arrived. So I watch Victoria, waiting for her to
lash out at me. I helped in this betrayal. I'm a traitor to her.
But she doesn't lash out. She sits near the corner of the bed
and stares at the wall. Imprisoned in her home.

The scraping of a key pulls my eyes towards the door.

I back up near Victoria. They've been torturing her. I ask why when they drag her out of the room. But no one says a word. When she returns, she stays silent...fuming, tired and silent. Roman steps through the doorway. My heart pounds. I haven't seen him since the betrayal. I've asked the soldiers, begged them to let me see him or Marina, but they ignore me.

"Abigail," he says, holding out his arms.

I start forward, and Victoria grabs my wrist. I turn towards her. She slowly shakes her head, her eyes trained on Roman.

"Traitorous bastard," she growls.

Roman steps back for a moment his handsome face registers sadness then just as quickly his lips break into a devilish smile. He slowly claps as he moves forward.

"Yes, I suppose I am."

"Wait, what is going on here?" I say looking between the two of them.

"Abigail, I came here to thank you. The Chancellor also wants to thank you for a job well done."

"What?"

"Yes, you see you were a vital part of bringing the high and mighty Victoria Cane to her knees."

"That wasn't my intention," I stammer.

"Oh, it wasn't? What about getting close to her, making

her trust you by pledging to be *Chusei*. Stealing her most precious information so that you could escape the Bright City."

"I never stole from her."

"No, no, she freely gave you the contacts. You were her pet project. She was molding you into the greatest Broker the Bright City had ever seen…well, that is, next to her."

"I don't understand."

"Oh yes, I know you don't. Just like I don't understand why you turned your back on your best friend when she begged you to see that your father is evil!"

"I never turned my back on Katherine!"

"Our surveillance says otherwise."

"What surveillance?"

"You had the disc. Katherine passed it to you."

"It was stolen from me."

"Yes, and of course we had to figure a way to sneak you out of the Colony. We had to sacrifice Katherine's life for yours because you couldn't be bothered to show up until a month had passed! She waited for you. She promised us that you would come through. She said you would never let her rot under that bastard, Warren Peters. She was wrong. In the end, she made us choose you; even after you betrayed her. She believed in you. But look at you; you are a traitor to everyone who loves you. Katherine *and*

Victoria. You might've even betrayed Marina or me if it would've suited your needs."

"Wait, I don't understand. Katherine didn't have to die?"

"Someone had to die. Katherine just didn't want that someone to be you. She sacrificed her place in the Bright City for her best friend," Roman says.

"Her place in the Bright City?"

I turn to Victoria then back to Roman. Roman is vibrating; he would spring on both Victoria and me if he could. Something is holding him back. I take in everything he said. I did abandon Katherine, but I would never do that now. I know too much. I could never see her as a rebel. She was trying to show me that our society was thick with deception. Back then I was a loyal soldier. I wouldn't have heard her. Even if I could have seen everything on that disc, I probably wouldn't have believed her. Now I understand treachery. Now I know what it's like to be a traitor and to be deceived by someone I love. They were wrong to exile me. I wouldn't have turned against my father. But I would have also never turned against Katherine. She sacrificed her life so that I could live? And Roman is standing here talking about Katherine as if he knew her. My mind whirls around the moving pieces. I think back to the pit, all the bodies in the crater, the deal the soldier ranted about making. Then to Victoria creating a huge distraction to steal me. But why choose me? Who was I to her but just another young girl forced into an arranged marriage? I try to fit the pieces together. Is it possible that none of this is a coincidence? Is it possible that my charmed life is just a part of the pieces moving across an invisible board? I still can't see the connections, but I feel like I'm getting close. For the first time in days, my mind shifts into gear. My training kicks in; I begin to analyze the situation, furtively searching for all the end goals. If I want to find out everything I have to fake brokenness. I'm back in the game.

"Do you think that you were 'saved' by Victoria just because she has a big heart? She's not that generous," Roman says.

"Don't you dare! I demand to see the Chancellor," Victoria yells.

"Shut up," Roman growls, "the Chancellor does not have to honor *deals* with Prolets."

"Deals," I ask.

"Ah, yes, you are a deal. Your existence, your very life is all a deal."

"Roman, I don't understand," I beg.

"Ask your mentor, she knows all about deals. Making them and breaking them."

"The Chancellor will honor our deal," Victoria says in a voice too calm for the tension in the room.

"Ha! Not with you. By the way, your rebranding is tomorrow evening."

"Rebranded," I ask.

"Yes, your mentor here had a little cosmetic surgery a few years ago. The Chancellor overlooked it. The

Chancellor sometimes ignores those few who slip through. The whisper of the expensive and painful de-branding that an ambitious Prolet can procure with the right sponsorship."

"The Chancellor is my sponsor."

"No, the Chancellor *was* your sponsor."

"I thought Prolets couldn't rise into the Uppers."

"You see the lies she's told you? Well, it's a good thing you betrayed her."

I sit down on the edge of the bed. Out of the corner of my eyes, I watch Victoria pace just out of Roman's reach. I see her flinch when he sits down at the small table near the door. It is nearly imperceptible, but it's there. I realize he's the one that's been torturing her. Now he's doing it in front of me. I have to get him out of the room. I may have betrayed her, but I will not have him play mind games with her. My heart breaks just a little.

"Brand me," I whisper.

"Excuse me, speak up, Abigail," Roman sneers.

"Brand me," I say standing in front of him, blocking his view of Victoria.

"Ha! No, no the Chancellor will not go for that."

"I'm the traitor."

"Yes, yes you are, but we have a plan for you, and we can't have you marked, at least not just yet."

BRIGHT CITY

"I don't want to be a part of plans anymore."

"You don't have a choice, *Vice Regent*."

It has been two years since anyone called me that. I cringe at the entitled sound of the words. What I had come to know is that my Colony is corrupt. My father is corrupt, and I was a part of that corrupt system. We were prisoners in a utopia. The very thought is ironic. Morbid. Maddening. I've learned that I could never go back there. More importantly, I never want to go back there. But now I see the plan coming to fruition with Roman's contemptuous sneering of my title. I see it. They're planning to send me back. But to what and to what ends?

"I'm no longer a Vice Regent. I'm a Broker. I am *Chusei*."

"You can't send her back. The Chancellor would never send her back," Victoria says.

"For two of the top Brokers in the Bright City, you two are about as dim as the lights in the Outlands. It's the Chancellor's idea to send her back. Of course, with a few modifications."

"Modifications?" I ask.

"No," Victoria whispers.

"Yes, you will be initiated into the Kaiji, a full brain wipe."

"No," Victoria's voice rises.

"It's not painful, but it will relieve you of everything

The Chancellor doesn't need you to know."

"No," Victoria screams and pounces on Roman.

Pushed aside by her momentum I fall back into a corner. Victoria beats Roman as an alarm blares around us. I manage to pull her off of him before the running thump of boots bursts through the door.

"You are going to die for that," Roman screams.

"No, she can't! She was just trying to protect me," I yell.

Two men grip Victoria as they drag her out of the room.

"Roman, you tell the Chancellor if she wipes her daughter's brain, I'll kill her."

Her daughter? Me? What? What did she mean? My vision is hazy as I see Roman wipe his bloodied nose with a white handkerchief. He straightens the collar on his cassock.

"Now that she's out of the way, your mother would like a word with you."

"My mother?"

"Yes. It's time for you to meet the Chancellor."

CHAPTER TWENTY-EIGHT

ॐ•ॐ

THE APEX TOWER WALLS GLEAM LIKE one of
Victoria's pearl necklaces. The air tastes fresh and
sanitized. It reminds me of home. Flanked by two
Kaiji, they lead me down the hallway, and I take glimpses
out of the floor to ceiling windows as we stride past them. I
hear the venting compressors quiet whir as it renews the air
around us. I've never been this close to the sun. The rays
spill onto the long white hallway; tiny rainbows dance
amongst the rays.

"Will I see Victoria again," I ask.

"Who knows," Roman says over his shoulder.

"Where's Marina?"

"So many questions. What you should be asking is
what is going to happen to you."

"What is going to happen?"

"The Chancellor will tell you."

"My mother is dead, you know."

"Yes, that is what your father told you. But he can't be trusted."

"And she can be?"

Roman whirls on me, grabbing my shirt between his fists and pushing his face close to mine. I smile. He grimaces.

"The Chancellor should have killed you when she had the chance, but she has a soft spot for you. I don't. You will not disrespect her…ever."

"I doubt she'd want you to rough me up so get your goddamned hands off of me."

The two Kaiji with us pull at Roman's arms, and he pushes them off straightening his jacket. He's a hot head. He never revealed that to me before. The two Kaiji nudge me forward, but this time they don't hold my arms. At the end of the hallway, Roman places his hand on a placard that comes alive with green where his fingertips press into it.

"Welcome to the Command Center," Roman says, as the doors slide open.

I step through the door. I feel transported back to the Colony. The Command Center looks like home. The Kaiji at my sides stay by the door as I walk to the center of the room. Everyone ignores me. I know this place intimately. I know what most every light signal and every button controls. I grew up in this room. But I tell myself as I slowly move from desk to desk that this is not my Command Center. We are not in my Colony; we are not in my Kingdom. I look up at the entrance and see the Kingdom mantra stenciled across the top of its doorway: Kingdom, Colony, and Family.

I watch two men step out of Comm Pods that look like the ones we use at home. All around me the young men and women wearing the navy colored uniforms of my Kingdom converse about the Outlands, the Bright City, and me. I stare in awe at three women who manipulate large holographic maps, moving and removing parts, throwing the discarded pieces of the hologram away like it's paper. I walk over to one of the unoccupied larger screens. When I lean in, I notice it's flipping through images. Then I realize the images are moving. But they're not pictures; they're videos. I touch my hand to the screen when it flips to a familiar looking place. The camera is pulled back so that I can't see the faces of the two men in the room. I make sure no one's looking before I grab the earpiece attached to the side of the viewer.

Do you know where she is?

No, I don't.

I told you to make sure that she got away.

She is lost to you. She was lost to you when she defied you.

She did what she thought was best.

She challenged your authority. You have to maintain control.

Control? I sacrificed my daughter to stop my wife from revealing the truth about…

"You don't need to hear this," Roman says, snatching the earpiece out of my ear.

"Wait, what the hell was that? Was that my father?"

"We have eyes everywhere. C'mon."

"No, tell me. Was that my father," I yell, pulling my arm from his fist.

"You don't get to ask any questions. You spoiled insolate brat. You don't get to hear any answers from me! You helped get Katherine killed. As far as I'm concerned you are beneath The Chancellor, beneath this crusade; you are just like your father…a murderer!"

"Roman!"

We both turn towards the voice. I suck in my breath. She looks like my mother. But not like my mother. My mother didn't have wrinkles around her almond shaped brown eyes. My mother was taller, but of course, I was shorter back then. Her ebony skin is smooth, but there are streaks of gray in her twisted braids. The withering look that she's giving Roman and me is familiar; there is no denying who she could be.

"Mom?"

I wonder why I'm numb. No tears, no thundering

heartbeat. No happiness. My mother who I mourned is in front of me. Her memory is like a shadow. I want to reach out and touch her; I want to see if she's real.

"Hello, Abby, welcome home."

She opens her arms, and I fall into them. Her scent is the same, cinnamon musk. She wraps her arms around me. I can't hear anything but my heartbeat. We pull away from one another. She rubs her fingers against my cheek.

"What happened to you? Dad said you were…"

"Dead. Yes, to him I am."

"I don't know…I have so many questions."

"We have plenty of time to talk."

I follow her as she turns towards a raised dais in the middle of the room. The furniture reminds me of the Council desks in the Mediation chamber.

"I need to find out about my friend, Victoria."

"Oh now you care about friends," Roman scoffs.

"What is with you and Katherine," I whirl towards him, rage spilling into my words, "How could you have possibly known her? Katherine was my best friend, and I have enough guilt over her death so screw you!"

"Stop it you two," my mother yells, "You are going to be working together from now on, so you must get along."

"What the hell is going on here," I say, sinking to the

floor.

My mother bends down next to me, her warm hand on my shoulder.

"I will tell you everything. But you have to trust me. And I know that's asking a lot because this all seems like we lied to you."

"Who should I trust?"

"When we talk, and you see everything we have gathered about the Kingdom, you can make your decision then. But for now, know that no one will hurt you ever again."

I force myself to relax into her embrace. But I know I can only trust myself. I have to use the skills Victoria taught me to survive. I am a survivor.

"Chancellor! Chancellor! We have a problem!"

"What is it?"

"The woman, Victoria, we were taking her to the implanting station…"

"Yes?"

"She escaped. Her and the other woman, Marina. They're gone."

"Damn it," Roman says.

"Find them, and when you do, execute them!"

EPILOGUE

THE LIGHT AHEAD PUSHES ME TO KEEP running. I lost the Searchers a week ago. But I remain hyper vigilant. At my side, Victoria doesn't look well, but I drag her along. We stop too often. She hasn't spoken since we were locked up in one of the bedrooms in her apartment. She never wanted to come back to the Outlands. Not like this. Now she's an exile like me. When we stop at night, I try to talk to her. But she's silent. She never looks at me. She stares off into the darkness or at the stars. I've apologized more than once. She has some apologizing to do too. She never told me her mission was to get me for my mother, the Chancellor. My mother who I thought was long dead is the Chancellor of the Bright City. She wanted to murder Victoria. She used her, then cast her aside. Kind of like my father throwing aside Katherine. I managed to steal some information, though. And when we get to Colony Four, I'm going to find out what all of the stolen data. That is if they let us in.

Large concrete walls loom ahead of us. I push us harder. We lost our cycle in a firefight with Kaiji soldiers a couple of weeks ago. They were the last ones following us. I wonder what Cleary and Roman are doing now. Cleary will have to report back to his father empty-handed. I hate that for him. Despite him trying to force me back to Knute, I know he's a good man. As for Roman saying he was in love with Katherine; I still haven't processed that information. Katherine kept a lot of secrets. More than I ever thought we'd have between us. Sometimes, I think about Marina. I wonder where she is. When I found Victoria in the cells below The Apex Tower, I couldn't find Marina. Those cells back home are part of the Re-Education Center. In the Bright City, they're just jail cells, intent on breaking the prisoner. I guess they're one in the same.

About 20 feet away from the steel doors, I do a quick scan of the area. Colony Four still looks active, even more than Colony One, my home. To the left about a mile away I see an Outlander settlement. Cooking fires and music drift across the wind. My stomach growls as the scent of roasting meat make my mouth water. We've been eating lentil paste and jerky. A warm meal would be good right now. There are what looks like Retribution soldiers at the gates and all along the tops of the walls. Highly guarded. Openly guarded. Being discreet isn't going to work, and we might get shot on sight.

I pull Victoria in the direction of the Outlander settlement, and we arrive just as the sun begins to set. I wrap us both in plain scarves, so only our eyes show. We slowly move through the marketplace. I try to see the currency is amongst the vendors. I ruffle through my pockets for the few coins I saved from Knute, smooth wooden pieces with copper etching. Cleary told me that several different Outlander clans use the coins. But I didn't know if those clans traveled this far southwest.

BRIGHT CITY

I stop at a food vendor to watch him do exchanges when Victoria nudges me. I turn to see some Retribution soldiers headed in our direction. My heart pounds as I try to pull us away. I run right into a traveler; my scarf falls away from my head as I crash to the ground. The soldiers stand over me, one of them holding Victoria.

"Ma'am are you alright," one of the Retribution soldiers, says to the traveler as another one pulls me up; gripping my arm until it almost goes numb.

"Of course," the traveler says.

"What do you want us to do with these two?"

"Bring them to the Command Center. We have a lot to discuss," the traveler pulls back her scarf. She is older than the last time I saw her. And I'm reminded it's been nearly four years. But if she's here…

"Harper?" I gasp.

"Welcome to Colony Four, Vice Regent."

Made in the USA
San Bernardino, CA
27 May 2017